DATE DUE			

Mermaid
KINGDOM

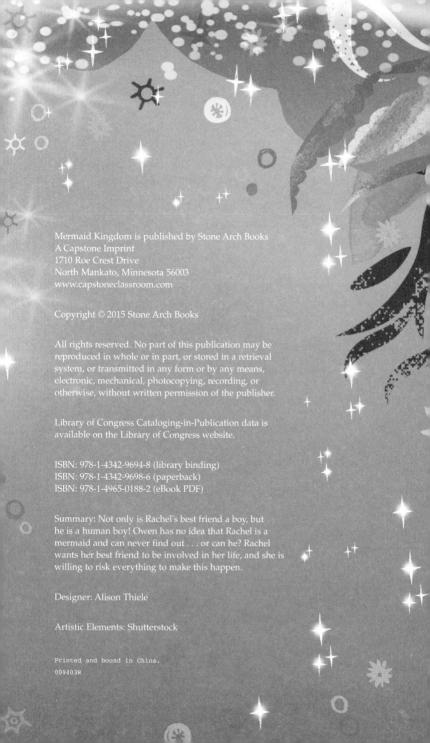

Mermaid Kingdom is published by Stone Arch Books
A Capstone Imprint
1710 Roe Crest Drive
North Mankato, Minnesota 56003
www.capstoneclassroom.com

Library of Congress Cataloging-in-Publication data is
available on the Library of Congress website.

ISBN: 978-1-4342-9694-8 (library binding)
ISBN: 978-1-4342-9698-6 (paperback)
ISBN: 978-1-4965-0188-2 (eBook PDF)

Summary: Not only is Rachel's best friend a boy, but
he is a human boy! Owen has no idea that Rachel is a
mermaid and can never find out . . . or can he? Rachel
wants her best friend to be involved in her life, and she is
willing to risk everything to make this happen.

Designer: Alison Thiele

Artistic Elements: Shutterstock

Printed and bound in China.
009403R

Rachel's Secret

by Janet Gurtler

illustrated by Katie Wood

STONE ARCH BOOKS
a capstone imprint

Mermaid Life

⭐ Mermaid Kingdom refers to all the kingdoms in the sea, including Neptunia, Caspian, Hercules, Titania, and Nessland. Each kingdom has a king and queen who live in a castle. Merpeople live in caves.

⭐ Mermaids get their legs on their thirteenth birthdays at the stroke of midnight. It's a celebration when the mermaid makes her first voyage onto land. After their thirteenth birthdays, mermaids can go on land for short periods of time but must be very careful.

⭐ If a mermaid goes on land before her thirteenth birthday, she will get her legs early and never get her tail back. She will lose all memories of being a mermaid and will be human forever.

✪ Mermaids are able to stay on land with legs for no more than forty-eight hours. Any longer and they will not be able to get their tails back and will be human forever. They will lose all memories of being a mermaid.

✪ If they fall in love, merpeople and humans can marry and have babies (with special permission from the king and queen of their kingdom). Their babies are half-human and half-merperson. However, this love must be the strongest love possible in order for it to be approved by the king and queen.

✪ Half-human mermaids are able to go on land indefinitely and can change back to a mermaid anytime. However, they are not allowed to tell other humans about the mermaid world unless they have special permission from the king and queen.

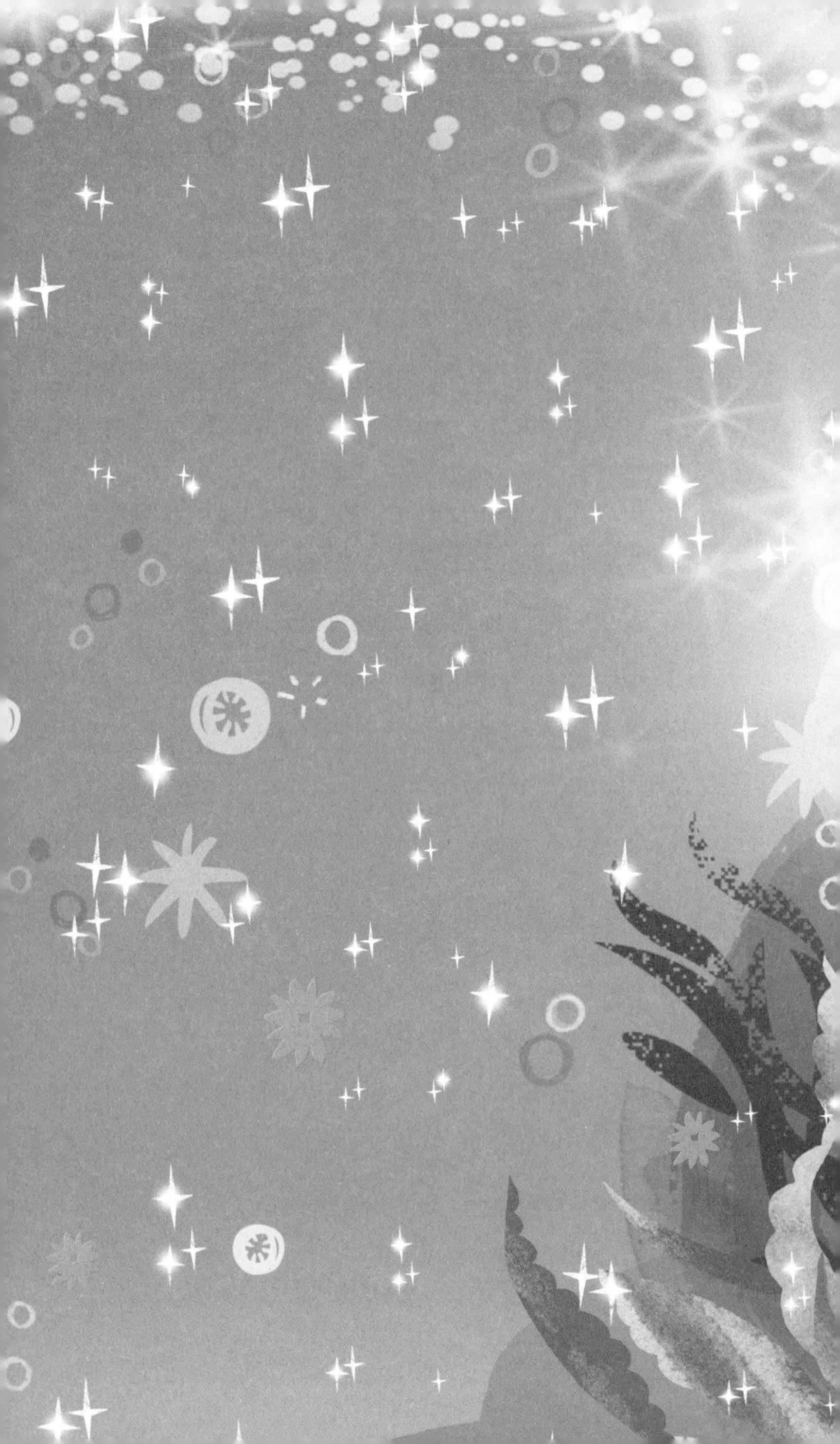

Chapter One

Shyanna and Cora were chasing each other around, laughing so hard that tears were falling down their rosy cheeks.

"Come on, Rachel!" Shyanna shouted to me.

My friends flipped in circles, swishing their glorious sparkling mermaid tails behind them. I smiled from the swing where I sat watching them, loving my two new friends with all my heart.

"Remember when, at your twelfth birthday party, you tried to convince Alexa you were thirteen?" Cora asked Shyanna. She looked at me and explained, "Alexa almost went to shore to see Shyanna's legs."

"Oh, I still feel terrible about that," Shyanna said.

"Only because you got in so much trouble!" Cora added.

They both giggled, and I had to admit that a teeny part of me felt left out. I was new to Neptunia. After my mom died, our entire life changed. My dad and I needed a new start, and moving to Neptunia was just what we needed. We'd just moved here.

I was lucky to have two best friends already, but it didn't make everything perfect. I missed my old best friend, Owen, every day. Sometimes I even missed living in Caspian and being closer to land. It was easier to go to shore and meet up with Owen from there.

Yep, Owen was a human. And having a human as a best friend had its challenges, especially since he didn't know that I'm a mermaid. Confused yet? Here's the deal: My mom was human before she became a mermaid. My dad fell in love with her when he spent time on shore. Because their love was so strong, she was given special permission from the King and Queen to become a mermaid and marry him. I was half-human. I could go on land whenever I wanted for as long as I wanted. It really was an incredible love story.

Shyanna was the only one who knew my big secret, and I intended to keep it that way. It was hard enough being the new mermaid in Neptunia. I couldn't even imagine how freaked out the other mermaids would be if they knew I was half-human!

"I can't wait for my real thirteenth birthday," Shyanna said as she twirled around. "I can't wait to get my legs! My leg ceremony is going to be so great!" Her eyes opened wider, and she glanced at me. "I mean, the ceremony is only part of it. Having legs and visiting land will be the best part."

I knew she was trying to make me feel better. I wouldn't have a legs ceremony on my thirteenth birthday. Since I was half-human, I already had my legs. I could go on land whenever I wanted for as long as I wanted. No matter what, I'd always be a little bit different. I knew it was okay to be different, but that didn't make it easy.

I didn't even bother to tell Cora and Shyanna that my thirteenth birthday was the next day. It wasn't the big deal it would have been if I were a real mermaid, so I didn't want them to know.

Cora swam over to the swings and floated around me. "Hey, you! There's no need to look unhappy when you could be playing tag with us!" Cora squealed. She grabbed my arm and playfully pulled me off the swing. "Come on, I need your help! Shyanna gets a little crazy when we play tag."

I couldn't help laughing and dashed after Shyanna with her. It was hard to stay miserable for long with my two new friends. I raced after Shyanna, but Cora ended up catching her first. Cora was the fastest swimmer I'd ever seen!

We were still laughing when a royal trumpeter and messenger swam into Walrus Waterpark. We immediately stopped and floated at attention. The trumpet player lifted his trumpet to play the royal fanfare. A purple royal flag dangled from the middle of the trumpet as he blew out the royal tune.

When he finished, the messenger unrolled a scroll, cleared her throat, and began to read. "The Queen would like to invite Rachel Marlin, Cora Bass, and Shyanna Angler to appear with her in a Royal Concert," she announced. "Queen Kenna has requested you sing as her opening act a week from today in the Royal Gardens."

"Of course!" we all squealed in delight. That was an incredible honor! Our showstopping performance at the Melody Pageant had clearly not gone unnoticed by the Queen.

One of the reasons my dad and I had just moved to Neptunia was so he could be the Queen's singing instructor. That's how I met Shyanna and Cora. It's a long story, but I basically saved Shyanna, then she saved me, and then all three of us ended up singing together and becoming best friends. I guess the story wasn't that long.

"Wow!" Cora said. "I never thought I'd be invited to sing with the Queen!"

"It must be because of the Melody Pageant," I said. "She told my dad how impressed she'd been with us!"

Shyanna and Cora swam in little circles and shrieked with excitement again. Their energy was definitely contagious.

"My dad hinted that she might have a concert," I confided to them. "She's improved so much, and I think she wants to show off a little."

I hated to brag, but my dad really was the best singing coach in all the Mermaid Kingdoms.

"I have to get home to tell my sisters," Cora said. "They'll be thrilled — and jealous!"

"I need to tell my mom!" Shyanna said.

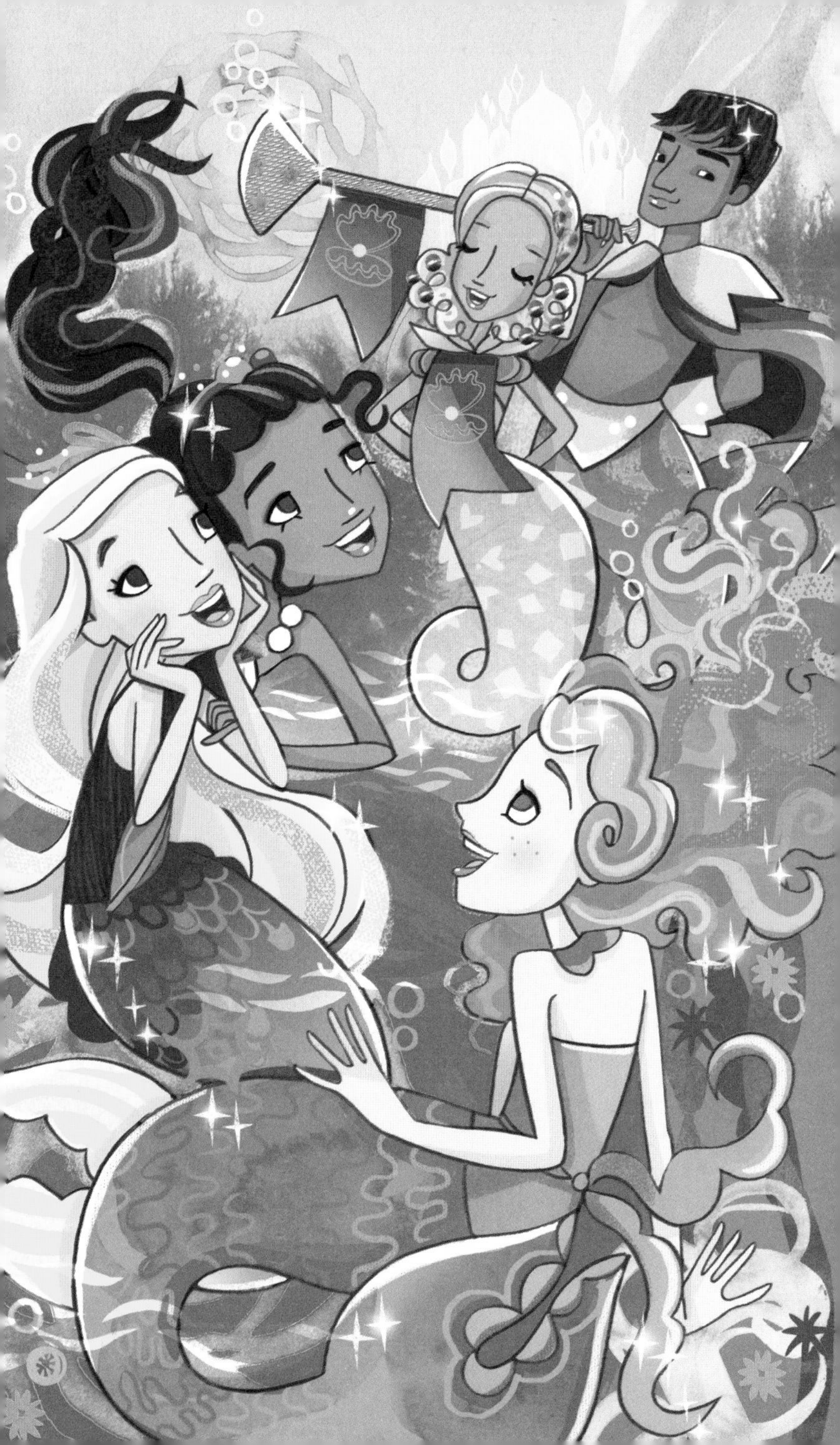

My dad already knew, and the only other person I wanted to tell was Owen. But I couldn't do that, of course. He didn't even know I was a mermaid. I wished so much that I could share my secret with him, but that wasn't possible, no matter how hard I wished.

Chapter Two

When I woke up the next day, my dad was already at work. I was a little disappointed that he was gone. It was my birthday, and I was all alone. However, he did leave me a nice note telling me to get ready for our fun day together. He was going to be home after lunch.

Dad and I had planned a father-daughter day. We were going to spend our time exploring out in the ocean. He'd been so busy since we'd moved to Neptunia. The Queen and her royal mermaids were all taking voice lessons, which took up a lot of time. We'd hardly had any time together.

I spent the morning braiding and beading my hair and polishing up my tail. I was so excited for our day together that I was waiting at the door for him to come home. But as soon as he swam inside, I could tell our plans were not going to work out.

He pulled a bouquet of flowers out from behind his back. "Happy birthday, Rachel. I hate to do this, but our plans have to change. I'll be home a little late, but we'll celebrate then. I promise I'll make it up to you." He could tell I was disappointed.

"That's fine," I said, but I didn't mean it.

"I'm really sorry, honey," he said. "The Queen requested an extra rehearsal this afternoon, and I couldn't get out of it."

"Thanks, Dad," I said. I was trying really hard not to cry.

"I wish we had planned you a party. You are thirteen, after all," he said, frowning.

"No," I told him. "I didn't want to make a fuss about it."

He kissed my forehead. "You're so much like your mother. She never wanted to have parties for herself either. Could you at least go see Shyanna and Cora? I'll be home with cake later. I'm so sorry."

"It's okay," I told him. "It's not your fault. You work for the Queen. We knew you'd be busy!"

He rushed back to work, and I called Shyanna. Her mom said she and Cora were at the waterpark with Cora's sister, so I swam over there. When I arrived, I saw them pushing Cora's littlest sister on the swings.

"Wow!" Shyanna said when she spotted me. "You look amazing! What's the occasion?"

"Not much," I said. "I was supposed to go out with my dad, but he's busy with the Queen for the rest of the day."

"Aww," Shyanna said. "That's too bad. I bet you were really looking forward to it."

She swam over to touch my hair. "How did you do that to your hair? It's so pretty."

"It looks incredible!" Cora agreed, and she swam over to check out my red braids.

"Cora, you should wear yours like that for your thirteenth birthday!" Shyanna said.

"Great idea." The girls fussed over my hair and admired the sparkles and glitter I'd added to my tail. But soon baby Jewel started to cry, so my friends swam back to the swings and started pushing again.

"I can't wait for my leg ceremony!" Cora said. "Mostly so I can go on land and get some peace and quiet for a few hours."

I smiled at her. Her life was so different from mine. She was always busy babysitting her sisters or helping her mom around the house. She rarely had time alone, which was something I had plenty of!

"I can't wait to have cake!" Shyanna shouted. "With oyster frosting!"

Cora laughed. "You always want to have cake."

"Yes. Like today is Friday. There should be cake!" Shyanna joked.

I smiled, but then it clicked. Friday!

When I lived in Caspian, Friday was the day I'd always gone to visit Owen. Now I realized I had the perfect opportunity. Who better to see on my birthday now that dad was busy with the Queen? It took longer to swim to shore to see Owen now that I lived in Neptunia, but I had extra time.

"Um . . . I have to get going," I said and somersaulted in delight.

"Where are you going?" Cora asked.

"Just back to my cave to relax," I said. I hated to lie to Cora, but I couldn't tell her the truth.

Shyanna and I exchanged a knowing look. I waved and smiled at them as I swam as fast as I could out of the waterpark. The sooner I could get to Owen, the better!

Chapter Three

I stumbled on the rocks and raced up the beach. My legs always felt a little wobbly and unsteady when they first changed over from my tail. I coughed, getting used to breathing in fresh air instead of filtering ocean water through my gills.

I was at the spot where I'd first met Owen. This was also the same place where Shyanna almost got her legs too early when she went searching for throat medication. This was the spot where I saved her and our friendship was established. This was truly one of the best spots in the world. So many incredible memories were made here.

"Hey, clumsy!" a voice yelled.

"Owen!" I jumped up and down, waving. I ran toward him, and even though I'm not a great runner, managed to get to his side quickly. I stopped, suddenly a little shy. "It's so good to see you."

"I had a feeling you were finally going to show up!" Owen said. "It's Friday! You always used to show up on Fridays." He stared at me for a second. "You look really nice."

"Thanks," I told him. "And sorry I haven't been here in a while. I've had trouble getting away."

Since my mom had died and we moved to Neptunia, it was a lot harder to see Owen. He didn't know why I couldn't see him as much, but he never questioned it. He was a good friend.

"Well, I'm glad you're back," he said. "Especially since it's your birthday!" He grinned and then started walking, gesturing for me to follow.

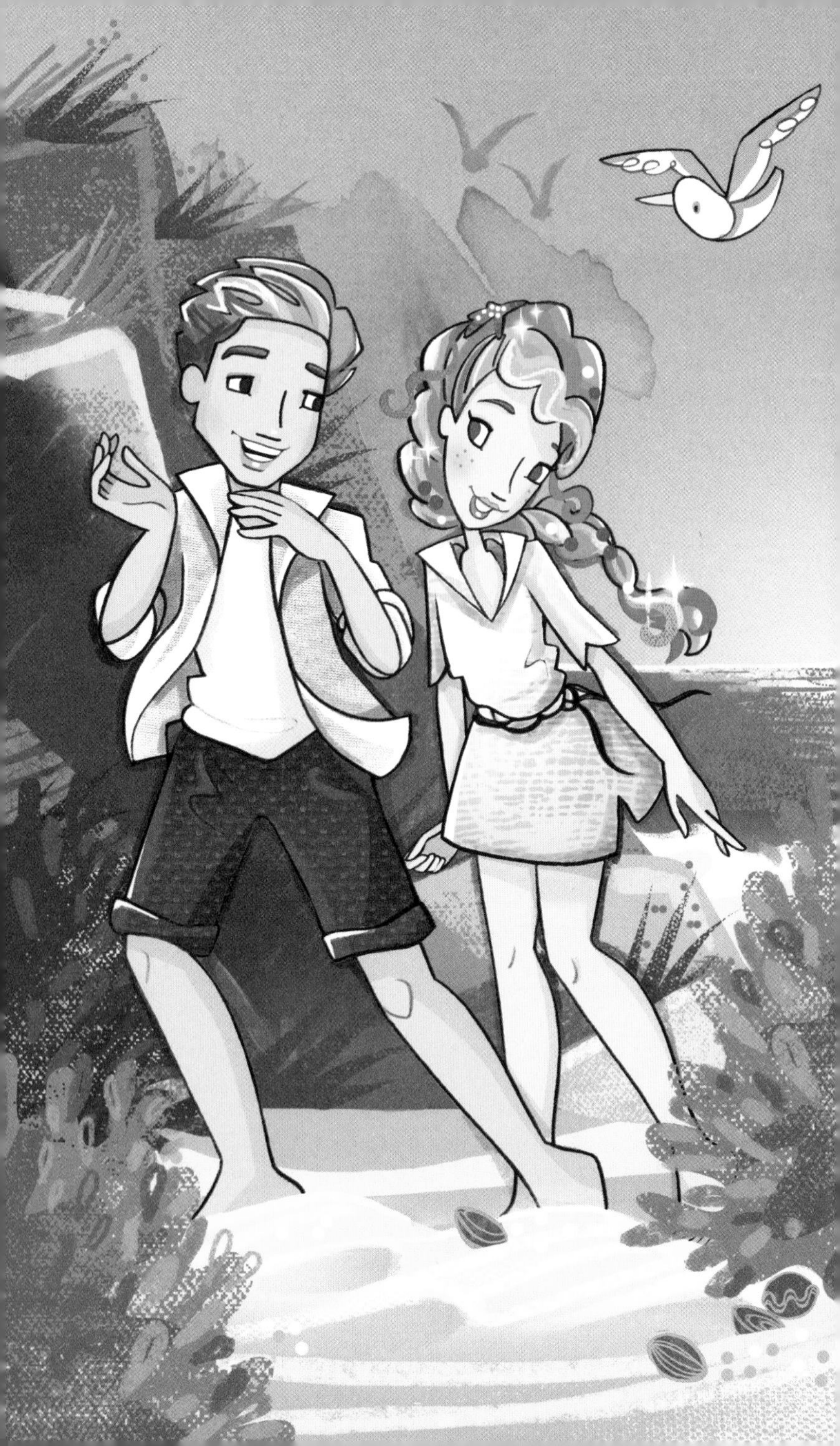

"You remembered?" I couldn't wipe the grin from my face as I scrambled to follow him.

"Of course I remembered!" he said, turning to me with his familiar sparkling grin. "Come on!"

"Where are we going?" I asked.

"My house," he said. "I had a feeling you'd show up, and I asked my mom to bake you a cake. Just in case. Don't tell the guys, but I think you're secretly her favorite friend of mine."

"She baked me a cake?" That made me so happy I almost cried. As we walked, I made a promise to myself to see Owen every Friday from now on. No more excuses.

"My mom loves you, and she loves baking cakes," Owen told me. "It was a win-win for her."

"She is the best!" I said.

"Justin, Mitchel, and Morgan are on their way over," Owen said. "They're at swim practice, but when they heard my mom made cake, they couldn't be stopped!"

His other friends were always nice to me too. It made me wonder why some mermaids are afraid of humans.

When we got to his house, his mom said, "Rachel! You're here!" Then she went into the kitchen and brought out the cake she had made.

She'd decorated the cake like a beautiful redheaded mermaid. My eyes bulged out of my head.

She laughed. "Don't you like it? I'm sorry. I only raised boys. I assumed all girls loved mermaids as much as I do! I've always wished they were real."

"Me too," I told her with a big grin. "I love it!"

The three boys barged in the front door then, just in time for cake.

Owen's mom put candles on the cake, lit them with a match, and they all sang "Happy Birthday" to me. We each stuffed ourselves with cake, and then Owen stood up and left the kitchen. He came back holding a pretty pink gift bag and put it on the table in front of me.

"A present? Is Rachel your girlfriend?" Morgan teased, grinning.

Owen's face turned red, and I felt my face get hot. I avoided looking at him when I reached inside the bag. I took out a box. Inside was a beautiful shell necklace.

"Do you like it?" Owen asked. "I can exchange it if you don't. Mom helped me pick it out."

"It's perfect!" I told him and immediately put it on. I decided I might never take it off.

His friends made embarrassing whistles and kissy noises.

"We're just friends," Owen said. He looked extra cute when he blushed. Not cute in a boyfriend way, either. He will always just be my best friend, which was all I wanted.

I wished I could stay longer, but I knew I should get back to Neptunia. I reluctantly thanked Owen's mom for the cake. "I have to get going. My dad will expect me home soon," I said.

"I'll walk you back to the beach," Owen offered.

He thought I lived in a house close by, and he never went farther than the edge of the beach with me. I had made it seem like my dad was super strict, because that seemed like the best excuse. I'd wait an extra five minutes to make sure Owen was gone, and then I'd slip back in the water and return to life in the sea. Thankfully Owen wasn't very snoopy, or things would fall apart fast.

"I wish you were around more," Owen said when we reached the edge of the beach. His cheeks were a little red again. "How come you aren't coming by as much as you used to?"

I stared at my feet. "I wish I could tell you," I whispered. "But you wouldn't understand."

I couldn't tell Owen I was a mermaid — or even half a mermaid. The secret was protected by mermaid magic. If I told him without special permission from the Queen or King, I'd never get my tail back and I'd have to live as a human forever.

After a few months without my tail, I'd forget that I'd ever been a mermaid at all. I knew the rules.

"Is everything okay?" Owen asked.

"Everything is great! I promise," I told him. "I have a couple of new mer . . . friends. And they're great. I'm busy. But I miss you too." Owen knew I'd had a rough year, but he didn't know I'd moved to a new Mermaid Kingdom. Obviously.

"You're sure?" he asked.

"Everything is great, I promise," I said.

"Okay," he said. "But remember . . . there's nothing you could tell me that would make me not want to be your friend."

I smiled. "Thanks, Owen," I said.

"Will you be back next Friday?" he asked. "I'm having a party at my house."

"It's your thirteenth birthday," I said, suddenly remembering.

But then I remembered that Friday was the concert too.

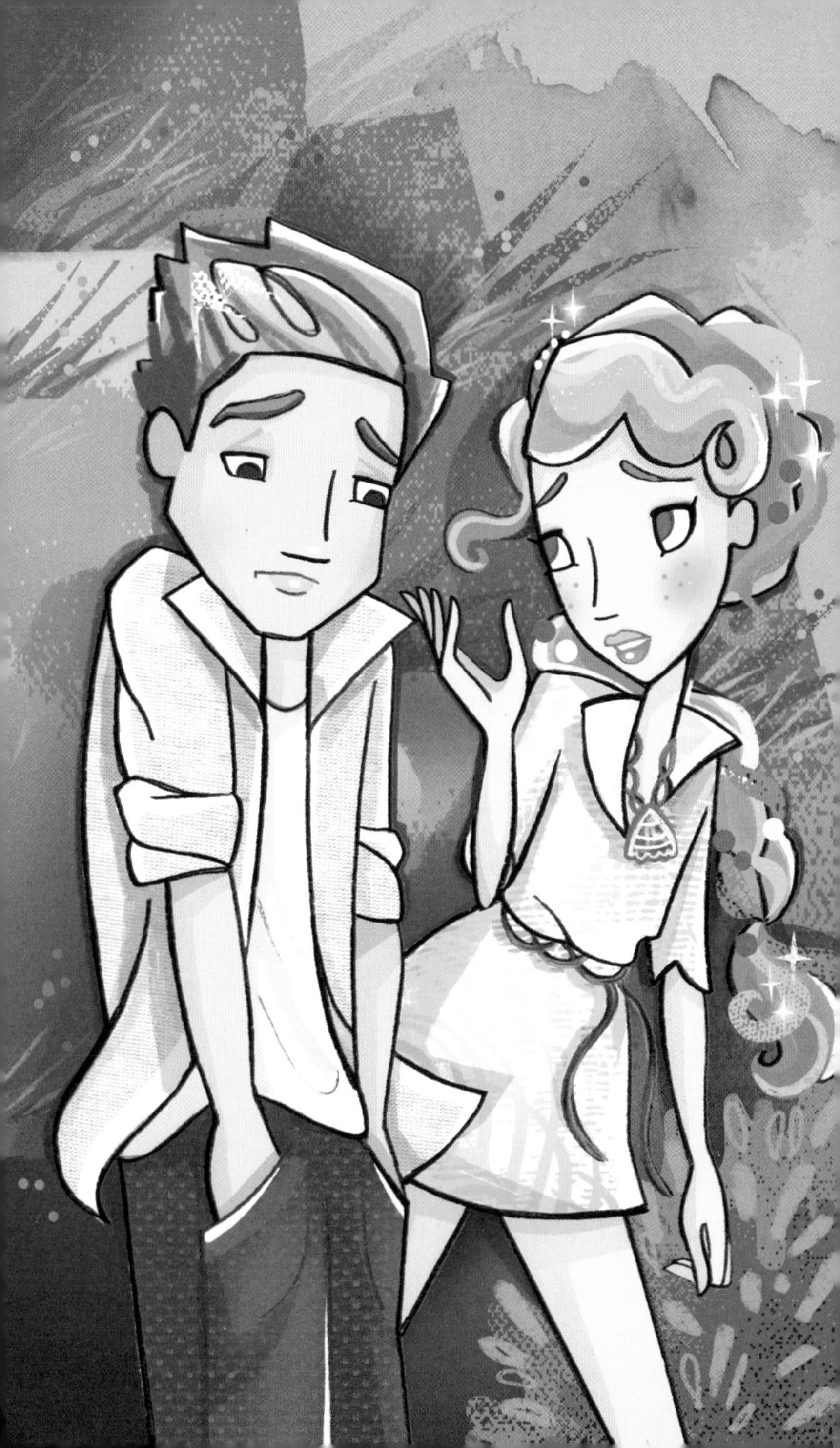

He looked at my face. "What's wrong?"

I dropped my gaze to my toes. "I can't believe it," I said. "I'm in a concert that night. Singing for the Queen — uh, I mean, someone really important. I'm committed to it. I'm so sorry." Telling Owen I couldn't be at his party felt worse than stepping on a stingray.

Owen ducked his head down. "No. It's okay," he said, but he couldn't hide his disappointment.

There was no way to back out of singing, but there was also no way I could miss Owen's birthday party. Especially when he went out of his way to make mine so great!

"I'll try to think of something," I told him.

What was I going to do?

Chapter Four

I swam quickly through the ocean, and even though I felt down about Owen's party, I couldn't help smiling at a group of lobsters and crabs who waved at me along the way. I really did love all the creatures in the sea, and they helped cheer me up.

The guards outside Neptunia nodded when I swam through the coral entrance. They were getting used to my coming and going.

When I darted inside the front door at home, Dad was sitting at the kitchen table.

"Rachel," he said. "Where were you?"

"Hi, Dad," I said. "I went to see Owen. I missed him more than I realized."

"I figured as much," he said. "But from now on, you need to let me know. I was getting worried."

"Sorry, Dad," I replied.

That's when I noticed a big cake sitting on the middle of the table. Thirteen unlit candles were stuck in the top.

"I feel terrible for messing up your birthday," he said. "I should have planned a party and had your friends over. I'm not as good at these things as your mom was."

"Well, I spent the day with my best friend, which made it great. Owen couldn't have come for a party anyway," I reminded him.

"I guess so." He patted my hand when I sat down beside him. "The Queen's cook made the cake when I told her it was your birthday. It's your favorite — shrimp-vanilla."

I didn't tell him that Owen's mom had made a cake too. And that it had been one of the most delicious ones I'd ever tasted.

He put his arm around me. "I'm sorry we didn't have a birthday celebration for you."

"It's okay, Dad. I had a great birthday. And I'd love a piece of cake," I said. Then I forced myself to eat a big piece even though I was already full.

* * *

The week flew by with lots of rehearsals and fun. Finally the night of the concert arrived. I was excited to sing, but I couldn't stop thinking about Owen and his party.

Shyanna had invited Cora and me to her house on Friday afternoon. Shyanna's mom made snacks while we got ready. I'd offered to help Shyanna braid her hair. She stared at my necklace as I braided the front of her hair.

"Hey! That's beautiful. Is that new? Where did you get it?" Shyanna asked.

"Um . . . I got it from a friend," I told her, and glanced at Cora.

Cora's hair was curled in beautiful waves, and she was glossing up her purple tail with fish oil. She wasn't paying attention to us.

"An old friend," I added quietly.

Shyanna's eyes opened as wide as sand dollars. "Owen?" she whispered, but she wasn't quiet enough.

Cora swam closer and stuck her face right up to mine. "Who's Owen? Is he your boyfriend?"

"No," I said, but my cheeks reddened like a lobster in boiling water. "I mean, he's a boy, and he's a friend. But he's not a boyfriend."

"Why did he buy you a necklace, then?" Cora asked, putting her hands on her hips.

"It was for my birthday," I said quietly. I moved behind Shyanna to admire my work.

Shyanna spun around. "Your birthday? When is your birthday?"

"It was last Friday," I admitted and patted her braided head. "Your hair is done," I told her. "It looks beautiful. It's your best look yet."

"You just had your birthday and you didn't tell us?" Shyanna said. She looked surprised, mad, hurt, and sad all at the same time. She knew my secret, so I was surprised by her reaction.

Cora flipped in semicircles. "You had your thirteenth birthday? You had a leg ceremony without us?" Her mouth hung open, and she looked hurt too.

Shyanna and I exchanged a look. "We'll make it up to her later," Shyanna said with fake enthusiasm. "Right now, we should practice our song!" She was trying to distract Cora. She belted out the first line of the song. I joined in, thankful when Cora stopped frowning and sang along with us.

"We're all ready to go!" Shyanna announced when we finished the song. She hurried us off to have snacks, and luckily, kept up the conversation about things other than my birthday until we left for the big concert.

When we arrived at the Royal Gardens, we all took a deep breath. It was transformed with a stage that looked like the inside of an oyster shell. Shiny colors and pearls were strung together and hung from a peach coral reef dripping with sea flowers. It was beautiful!

Other mermaids who'd been picked to sing with the Queen were fussing around behind the stage. Workers roamed around them, some carrying huge stage props. Somehow I got separated from Cora and Shyanna and was shoved into a tight space with a group of other mergirls from Neptunia. I recognized one mermaid named Regina. Shyanna had said she was the most popular girl in school.

Regina noticed me right away. "You're Mr. Marlin's daughter, aren't you? The Queen's new singing instructor?"

I nodded.

"I saw you sing in the twelve-year-old category at the Melody Pageant. You were really good," said one of the other mermaids.

"Thanks," I said and smiled at her.

Regina glared back at me. "When do you turn thirteen?" she asked, putting her hands on her hips.

"Um. I already did?" I said, wondering why she seemed mad at me. "Last Friday."

"But you never had a party?" asked Regina. "At least I never heard about it. And I hear about all the important parties in Neptunia."

"I had a party," I said right away. "It just wasn't in Neptunia."

"But how could you have your leg ceremony without Shyanna and Cora?" Regina asked. "I saw them at Walrus Waterpark last Friday. I thought they were your best friends. That seems . . . fishy."

My cheeks burned. I couldn't think of anything to say. I glanced around, wishing the workers would hurry up so I could get away. I wished Shyanna and Cora would appear to defend me and get Regina to go away. She was acting as if I'd done something wrong. I didn't even know her! I didn't know what her problem was.

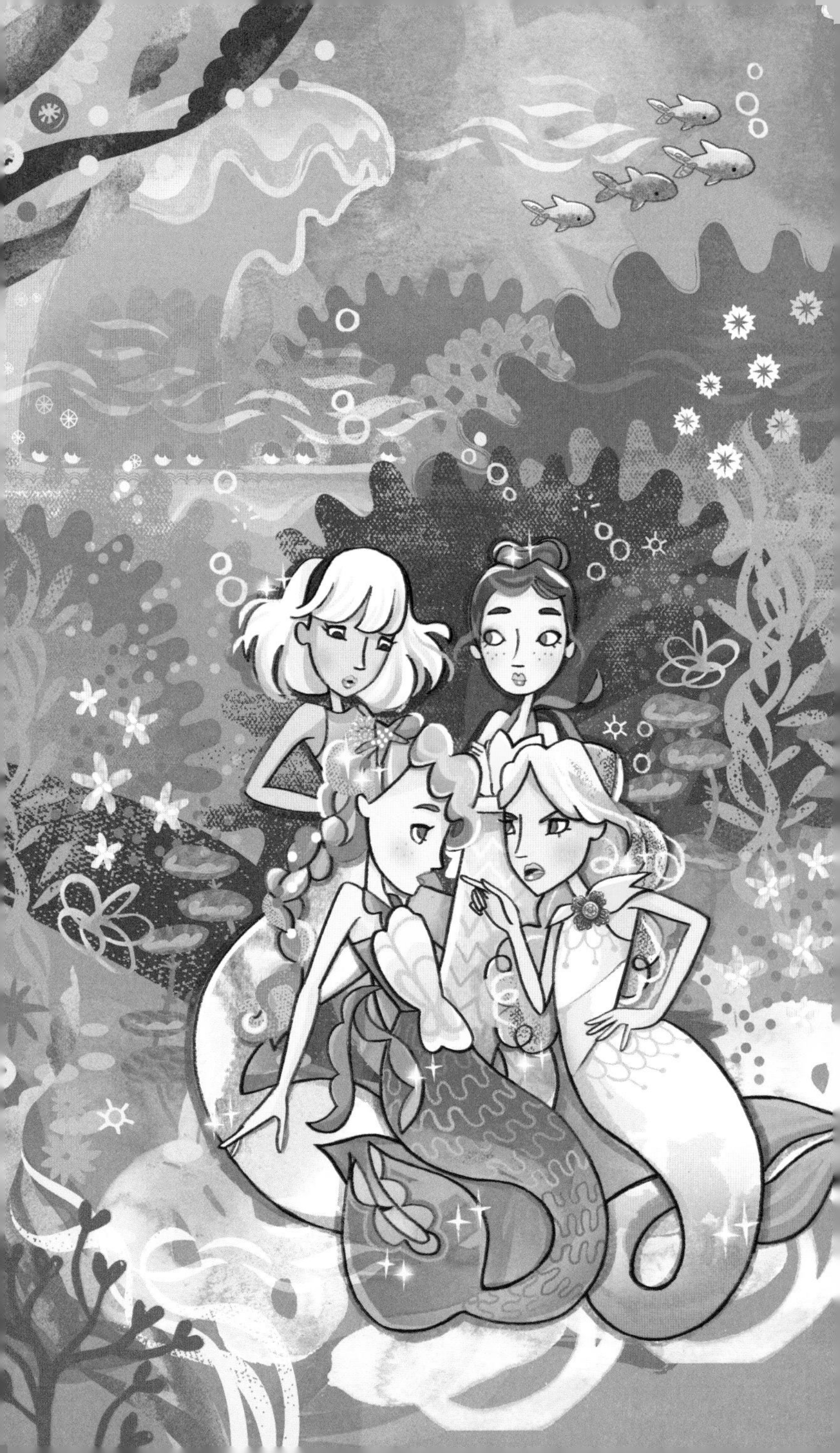

Then Regina narrowed her eyes. "You know . . . my mom heard a rumor. A rumor about your mom," she said with a smug look on her face.

I sucked in a deep breath. Oh no. Was she going to start teasing me because my mom was human and I was half-human? Some mermaids didn't approve of humans who became a mermaid by magic.

"My mom was amazing," I said, swallowing a lump in my throat.

"Regina," the nice mermaid said. "Her mom died. Don't be mean."

Regina wrinkled up her nose and moved away from me as if I smelled like three-day-old fish fries. "I only hope the rumors about your mom aren't true." And with that, she turned her back on me.

The nice mermaid smiled weakly at me, but turned back to the group. "Remember my leg ceremony? Everyone said it was the best one ever!" Regina said to her friends as she flipped her hair and batted her long eyelashes.

The other mermaids looked guilty, but they nodded. Finally the workers cleared out of the way, and the group swam off, Regina in the lead.

Just then, Shyanna and Cora swam over.

"There you are!" Shyanna cried. "We've been looking everywhere for you. We're on in five minutes! Can you believe it?"

"Are you okay?" Cora asked, looking closer at me.

"I'm fine." I faked a smile.

"I saw Regina," Cora said. "Was she being mean?"

"No, I'm fine," I told them again.

They looked like they didn't believe me, but it was too complicated to explain since Cora didn't know the truth yet. I knew I had to tell her soon, but I was waiting for the right moment.

An event worker came along and hurried us to the stage, and then, before I knew it, we were performing our song. It sounded pretty great. I felt like I was in a dream the entire time we were singing. And before I knew it, we were done.

It went by so fast! All of our hard work and practice had paid off. It was amazing how much music could still make me feel better.

After we finished, Cora and Shyanna hurried out to the audience to watch the rest of the show and help with Cora's sisters.

"Want to come along?" Cora asked.

I shook my head. "I'm going to stay here in case my dad needs help."

That was partly true. But I also had a plan.

Regina swam by to go on stage and looked right at me. "She's not even a real mermaid," she whispered to a friend, and both girls turned away from me.

I glanced at my dad behind the curtains. He was beyond happy directing the show and was totally in his element. I looked at my phone.

I wanted to see Owen so badly! If I left right away, I could make it to his party and be back before anyone missed me.

My dad had told me a hundred times that I needed to tell him when I was going to land, but he was too busy to bother right then. Plus, he didn't even have to know. I would be back before he even noticed I was gone.

I swam out of the Royal Gardens, and then out of the kingdom and toward the shore. When I got to land and grew legs, I hurried up the beach toward Owen's house.

Before I even reached Owen's backyard, I could hear the party. Owen's house was lit up with glowing party lights. Happy noises floated through the air. I went to the front of the house and was about to ring the doorbell to join the party when I heard noises and shouts.

"Last one in is a rotten egg!" someone yelled.

The thundering army of kids sounded louder than a sea storm. Everyone was running out through the backyard toward the beach, all of them wearing bathing suits. Owen led the pack, laughing, with

Justin, Morgan, and Mitchel at his side as they raced to the water. My heart sank. I went to watch them, knowing I couldn't go see Owen now. It was too risky being so close to the water. If I got any salt water on me, my tail would reappear.

Instead, I went as close to the shore as I could and watched from the shadows.

Owen and his friends were having so much fun. Owen looked so happy. He didn't look like he missed me at all.

I went back to his house to leave him his present. I'd braided seaweed into a necklace and attached a real shark tooth. I left his gift at the front door and then headed down the street to a quiet beach. I leaped back in the water, feeling like I didn't belong in either one of my worlds.

Chapter Five

In the morning, I was tired from all my sneaking around. Dad had to go see the Queen early to review her performances, and he'd told me to sleep in. I stayed in bed all morning, but before lunch, the doorbell started ringing and didn't stop.

"Hey, Rachel, I know you're in there," a voice shouted from outside. "Let me in, lazy bones!"

With a big sigh, I got up and swam to the front door. When I opened it, my jaw dropped.

Shyanna floated on the front porch, holding a giant bouquet of balloons shaped like sea creatures in one hand and a starfish-shaped gift bag in the other hand.

"Happy belated birthday, sleepyhead!" she cried. "Cora and I got these for you. She wanted to come too, but her sisters are sick and her mom wouldn't let her leave."

My heart filled with happiness. "You look like a one-mermaid party pack!"

Shyanna laughed. "Are you going to let me in?'

"Oh!" I opened the door, and she handed me the balloons and gift as we went inside. "Thank you so much!" I said. I tied the balloons to a chair in the living room and put the gift down on the table.

"I still can't believe we missed your birthday!" Shyanna said.

"It's okay. I mean, turning thirteen is not as big as a deal for me, because I already have legs." I sat in the chair with the balloons and grinned. Shyanna sat across from me.

"Still . . . it was your birthday! Everyone deserves to feel extra special on her birthday," she said, clearly making a valid point.

"I went to see Owen," I told her. "His mom made me a cake. And his friends came over."

Shyanna clapped her hands together. "I'm glad. He seems like a good friend. I wish I could have come! Will you introduce me to Owen when I get my legs? I've never met a human before!"

Before I could answer, the doorbell rang. I got up and floated over to the door. When I opened it, Cora was flipping around in circles. She tackled me immediately, hugging me and giggling. "My mom let me come. My sisters are all sleeping!"

Cora swam inside and pulled me along behind her. "Yay!" she said when she saw the table. "You didn't open our present yet. Open it now! Open it!" she cried.

The girls spun around while I opened the bag and pulled out matching bracelets made of black pearls and braided seaweed. "One for each of us!" Cora said. "Friendship bracelets for forever friends!"

We all slipped them onto our wrists and held them out to admire them.

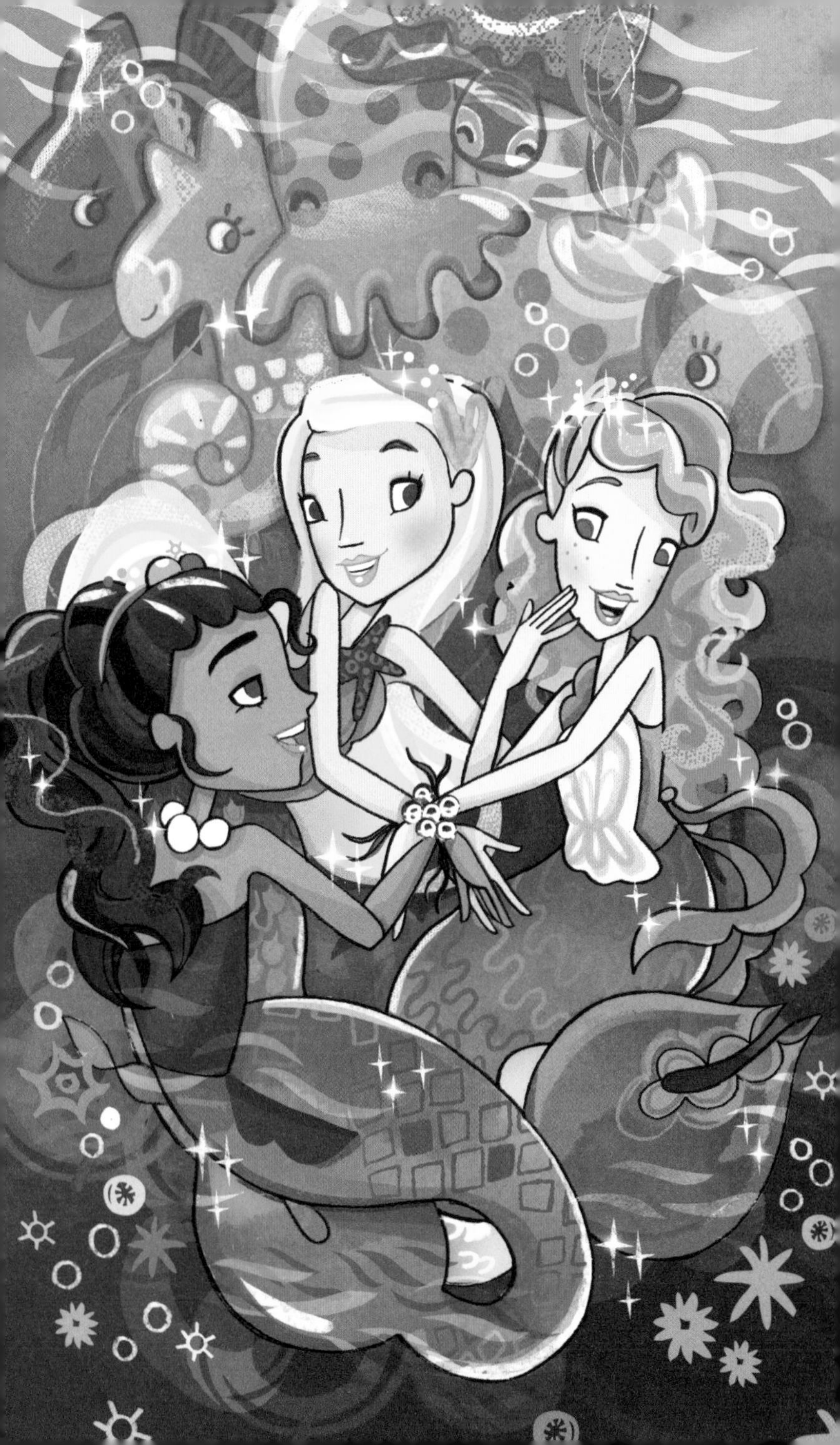

"They're beautiful," I said. "Thank you."

"So," Cora said. "I've been dying to know. Who's this Owen that you're so close with? You didn't think I would forget to ask you about him, did you?"

I glanced at Shyanna and then swam closer to Cora and took her hand. "I have a secret," I said. "Shyanna already knows because she caught me in the act, but I made her promise not to tell anyone."

Cora looked at me and then at Shyanna and then back at me, blinking. Waiting.

"I'm sorry I didn't tell you earlier. It's hard. I get teased," I said. "And I loved my mom so much, it's hard to talk about."

Cora grabbed my other hand. "What? What's wrong, Rachel?" Cora asked.

I took a deep breath and closed my eyes. "My mom was a human."

I waited for her to drop my hand or pull away in disgust or something.

"So?" she said.

I opened my eyes and started to laugh. "That's all you have to say? It means I'm half-human."

She let my hands go. "Oh. That doesn't matter at all." She opened her eyes wide and her mouth wider. "Wait. Does that mean you have legs? And that you can use them all the time?"

I nodded, and she stared at me without even blinking. "That is so cool," she said, in total awe. "It must be a romantic story, your mom and dad. Wouldn't it be amazing to fall in love with a human? How magical."

Shyanna cleared her throat, raised her eyebrows, and stared at me. I knew she was thinking about me and Owen.

"Stop looking at me like that, Shy. Owen and I are not in love," I told her. "We are just friends. Best friends — nothing more."

Cora looked back and forth between Shyanna and me. "Wait. What? Is this boyfriend of yours a human?" she asked me.

I touched the shell necklace Owen had given me. "A friend who's a boy. And yes. Owen is human. And he doesn't know I'm a mermaid."

"Wow!" Cora went to the table and sat across from Shyanna. "How did you meet a human?" They both stared at me, waiting for more information, I guess.

"Some of the mermaids from Caspian found out I was half-human, and they used to tease me. I went to land a lot to escape, and that's when I met Owen. At first, I was a little afraid of him, but he's so nice and adventurous. We quickly became best friends. I didn't have to worry about getting teased when I was with him. I used to visit him at least once a week, but I haven't been visiting as often since we moved to Neptunia."

"What's it like? To have a human as a friend?" Cora asked.

"He's great," I said. "He makes me feel like I matter, you know? I mean, he's like us. Only he doesn't get to enjoy the ocean like we do. I feel sad about that."

Shyanna and Cora nodded. I could tell they were both thinking how awful it would be not to enjoy the ocean like we were able to.

"The thing is, I've been away so much," I said. "I'm worried he's going to forget about me."

"He won't forget about you," Shyanna said, and Cora nodded in agreement.

"How could he?" Cora said.

"Thanks," I said, smiling and looking down at my friendship bracelet. "I got teased a lot in Caspian. The other mermaids were really mean. And Owen was so important to me. He still is. And the thing is, I think my secret is out again. I think one of the mermaids here knows about my mom."

"Who cares? The mermaids here won't tease you," Shyanna said confidently.

"I don't know," I said doubtfully. "The mermaid who hinted about it . . . she didn't seem too happy. I don't want everyone to look at me like I'm different. I hate being different."

"Who was it?" Cora asked, jumping up again. She had a hard time staying still.

"Regina," I said quietly.

"Regina Merrick? She can be really mean," Shyanna told me. "Was she being mean to you?"

Cora was pace-swimming around the room. I shrugged and looked away. "It doesn't matter. I'm tired of having to keep secrets from everyone," I said. "I hate hiding the fact that I'm a mermaid from Owen. It is awful. He is my best friend, and he has no idea what my real life is like."

"You're perfect," Cora said. "Just the way you are."

"I don't feel like it." I paused before I made my big announcement. The thing I'd been thinking about all night. "But I think I have a solution," I told them.

They both stared at me, waiting.

I stared back. Then, slowly, I said, "I think I might want to become human. All the time."

Chapter Six

Silence.

Complete silence. That's the response I got from my big announcement.

"I've thought about it a lot," I told them, slowly swimming toward the table. "It's not an easy decision to make."

Shyanna and Cora both looked shell-shocked.

"Why would you want to do that?" Cora asked quietly, frowning.

"It just seems easier," I said.

I plopped down in a chair, and we all faced each other in a circle. "You know how mermaid magic works," I said. "I would stay on land and not go near salt water for six months. After that, I would lose my tail. I could swim in the ocean, and it still wouldn't come back. And after I lost my tail, I would slowly start to forget that I'd ever been a mermaid. I would have memories of my life, of course, but it would all be kind of hazy. I'd believe I had always been human. End of story."

"You'd be willing to do that for a boy?" Cora asked, shocked.

"I wouldn't do this for a boy," I replied. "I would do this for me. I wouldn't have to feel like a freak anymore. I would be free from all the lies. I would be a normal person."

Shyanna started to cry. "But you would lose your beautiful tail," she said. "And what about all the wonderful parts of being a mermaid? What about exploring caves, looking for long-lost treasure? You'd never be able to talk to sea creatures again. And you would lose us."

"I would remember you," I said. "Just not all of it. And you could visit me once you have your legs."

Cora was up again, swim-pacing back and forth. "You wouldn't be able to race in the ocean. Or go to mermaid school or concerts. You wouldn't remember the King and Queen. You wouldn't remember the Melody Pageant. And what about your dad?"

I nodded. "I'd have to convince him to come with me. I could never leave him behind. I think he would do it. My mom was human. We could be too."

"I think that's about the saddest thing I've ever heard," said Shyanna. "We would miss you."

"You haven't even started school yet," Cora said softly. "And I really wanted you to join us on the Spirit Squad," she added. "But . . . it's also not right for mermaids to be sad."

Shyanna lifted her head to stare at Cora. "What are you saying, Cora?"

"I don't want her to leave," Cora said. Then she turned to me and asked, "But are you really that miserable and unhappy?"

I bit my lip and twirled my hair around my finger. "I love being a mermaid. And Neptunia is so wonderful. I'd miss you two so much." I paused, thinking how to say what I wanted to say. "It's just that . . . sometimes I feel left out . . . and so different from everyone else. And I'd really like to tell Owen the truth. He's always been honest with me, and he doesn't understand why I can't always be around. He was my first best friend."

"We're your best friends too," Shyanna said, her voice soft.

"I know. But Owen and I have a history. Like you two do," I explained.

"Being different isn't bad, you know," Shyanna said. "Who wants to be exactly the same as everyone else?" She was blinking fast, and her eyes were shiny with tears.

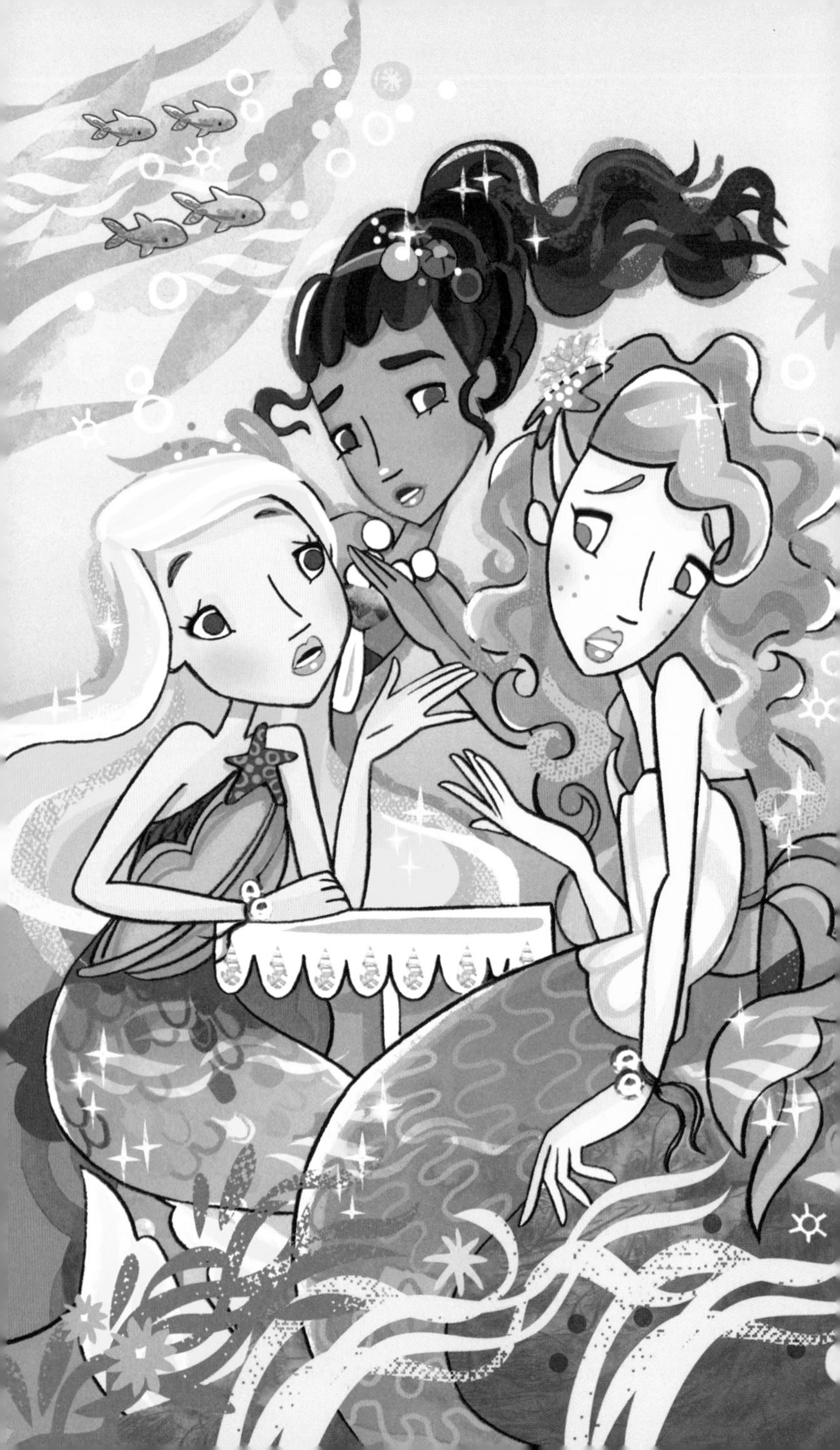

"Stay with us," she begged. "You'd be so unhappy never being a mermaid again. We'll come to shore with you as soon as we're thirteen. We can meet Owen when we get our legs. All of us can be friends. You can have both worlds if you stay with us. If you become human, that will be your only world."

Cora jumped up again. "We could make sure no one makes fun of you," she said.

I smiled at both of them. "You know I love you girls. But you can't always be around to protect me."

There was a noise from the front door. Dad swam inside. "Hey! Is there a party going on here without me?" He looked at Shyanna and Cora's faces. "Did I interrupt something? This looks like a serious party."

I glanced at my friends and shook my head slightly, pretending to zip up my lips so they'd know not to say anything.

"Not at all, Mr. Marlin!" Shyanna said. She tried to sound happy, but he frowned as if he suspected something was wrong.

"Listen, girls," he said. "The Queen wanted to let you know how thrilled she was with her concert — and you three, especially, for giving it such a good opening. She offered up her cook to make a special meal for us. Would you girls like to have dinner and then sleep over here with Rachel tomorrow night?"

Shyanna swam close and wrapped her arms around me tightly, hugging me like she'd never let go.

"We'd love to," Cora said, but her smile didn't last very long.

Dad frowned. He knew something was up.

Chapter Seven

After dinner, Dad sat down with me while I was putting clam juice in my hair to make it shine. "You wanted the girls to sleep over, didn't you?" he asked. "I thought it would be nice for you, but maybe I should have asked you first."

"Of course, Dad. It'll be great!" I ran my fingers through my hair to spread the juice around more evenly. "You know how much I love those girls. And having the Queen's cook make us dinner? Yummy!"

"I have a surprise before the girls come over," Dad said. "For the two of us. So don't make any plans."

"Okay!" I wasn't ready to have a serious talk

about becoming human yet, so I told him I was tired from all the concert excitement and went to my bedroom early that night.

I lay in my bed for a long time, staring up at my ceiling. The girls were seriously making me rethink my plan. I really did love being a mermaid. I loved the ocean and all the creatures, and I knew I'd miss everything I had to give up. Not only that, my dad would also have to give up the job he seemed to love so much.

The thing was, I suspected Regina was going to try to cause a lot of trouble for me. And I remembered all too well how hard it was to be made fun of all the time, especially when merkids also made fun of my mom. I missed her all the time, and I didn't care if she was part human or part penguin. I didn't want to hear anyone talking badly about her.

If only all the mermaids could accept me for who and what I was. I had Shyanna and Cora, but I'd always be the odd mermaid out. And what about

Owen? I didn't want to lose the first best friend I'd ever had.

I finally fell asleep, these thoughts drifting through my mind.

When I woke up in the morning, Dad was already gone. I played hide-and-seek with some clown fish in the morning, and in the afternoon, I played with some dolphins who came to visit. Life in the ocean really was magical. After a few more games, I headed home. Dad would be there soon. I had no idea what his surprise would be.

"We're going on an adventure, Rach!" Dad called when he finally got home from work. "You look like you need some cheering up, and I've been working far too much. Let's go have some fun! We both deserve it."

I nodded, trying not to look too guilty. I'd have to tell him my plans when we got home.

"I know you didn't get a big thirteen-year-old celebration like all the other mermaids, so we're going to have our own celebration before dinner," he said, grinning. "You and I are going to sing with the whales!"

"Really?" I gasped. That had been our favorite thing to do before Mom died. We would travel outside Caspian and call to the whales. The whales didn't usually sing with other sea creatures, but they could never resist joining in when they heard Dad and me singing together. Dad had taught me how to harmonize with the whales in a special key.

We swam out of Neptunia and kept going, the two of us bouncing in and out of waves toward the deepest parts of the ocean. Once we were in whale territory, Dad started to sing in his glorious voice. He soon signaled for me to join him, and before I knew it, sea creatures from all depths of the ocean came to watch.

We sang and sang, and dolphins and sea turtles danced around Dad and me, clapping their fins along to the music! Finally, it was time to leave. We bid farewell to all of our new friends and began to swim

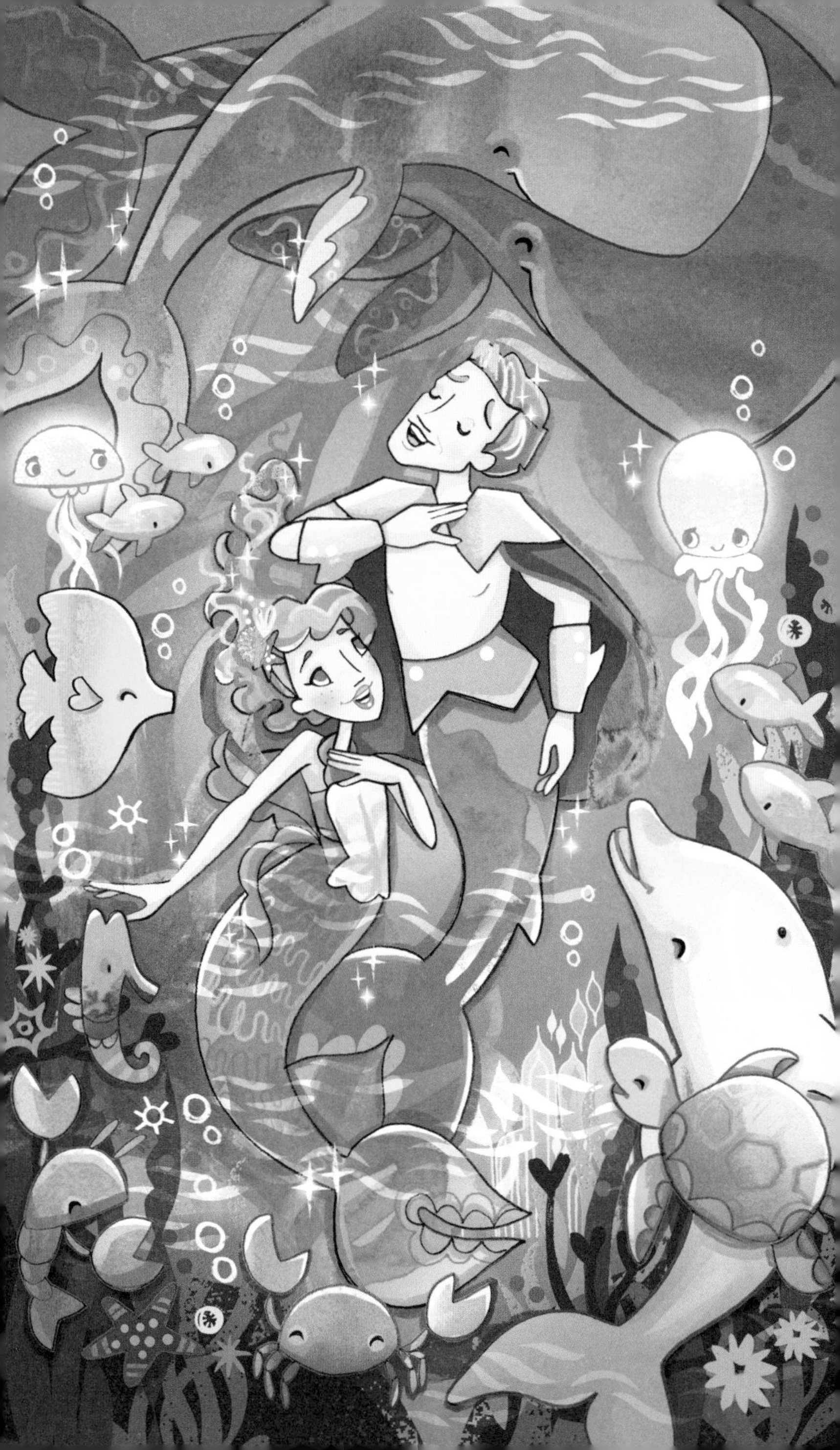

back toward Neptunia. On the way back, he stopped to show me a rare frost flower growing out of the ocean.

"Is everything okay, Rachel?" Dad asked me when we got home. "I want you to be happy. If you don't like it here, we can move again."

"Oh, Dad," I said. My eyes stung, and I thought I might cry. "You love it here, don't you? Working with the Queen?"

He swam to me and put his arm around me. "The main reason we moved here was so you would be happier. That's the most important thing to me."

I leaned against him. "I love Neptunia, Dad. I really do," I said. "And Shyanna and Cora are the best. It's just . . ."

"What is it?" He stared down at me with concern.

"I miss Owen. I'm afraid he's forgetting about me. I can't go and see him as much as I once did," I explained. "He was — I mean, is — my best friend. I feel like I'm losing him."

Dad nodded. He was a great listener.

"And, well, one of the mermaids found out I'm half-human," I said. "I have no idea how, but I guess it doesn't matter. I'm afraid the teasing is going to start up again. I don't know if I'll ever fit in, no matter what kingdom we go to. When mermaids find out about Mom, some of them don't like it."

His face turned red. "Who said something?" he asked angrily. "I will talk to her parents."

"No, Dad. You know that will only make it worse," I said.

He let go of me and swam in a circle, flipping his tail in frustration. "But it's not right. There has to be something we can do."

"Well," I told him. "Maybe there is something. I've been thinking about it a lot."

He tilted his head, waiting.

"What if we became human?" I asked softly. "I mean . . . what if we went to live on land? Forever."

Chapter Eight

Dad gasped. "You don't want to be a mermaid anymore?"

"I love being a mermaid," I said. "But I'm sick of being different. If we became human together, we would eventually forget our mermaid life. We'd fit in with the humans, and I could still keep Shyanna and Rachel as friends. They could come visit once they get their legs. I wouldn't remember that they were mermaids, but we could still be friends. All four of us — Owen, Shyanna, Cora, and me."

"That's really what you want?" Dad asked.

I nodded. "It wouldn't be so bad, would it? I mean, you must know a lot about being human from being married to Mom."

He hugged me again. "Being different is what makes us special, Rach."

"Sometimes it's hard being special," I admitted.

Suddenly, the doorbell rang, interrupting us. Shyanna and Rachel were floating at the door, arriving for the sleepover party.

"I know that." Dad sighed, looking a little defeated. "I'll do anything for you, Rachel. You know that. Let me see what I can do."

* * *

"Wake up, girls!"

I rubbed my eyes and looked at the clock beside my bed. It was early! Why was Dad waking us up? Didn't he know we liked to stay up as late as we could keep our eyes open at sleepover parties? Shyanna and Rachel were still sleeping on the floor beside my bed.

"Up and at 'em!" Dad called.

We all groaned.

"Come on. I'll make sardine pancakes for breakfast, but you'll have to eat them quickly. In the meantime, comb your hair, brush your teeth, and get ready!"

"Ready for what?" I asked, groggily. "Dad, sleepover parties don't end at seven in the morning. We still have things to do. We haven't even painted our fingernails or braided shells into our hair."

He tried really hard without Mom, but sometimes Dad really didn't understand girl rules.

"This is important," he said. "I talked to the Queen last night."

The girls rubbed their eyes. I frowned, asking him, "You did? When?"

"When I took the cook home last night after dinner," he explained. "I asked the Queen for a

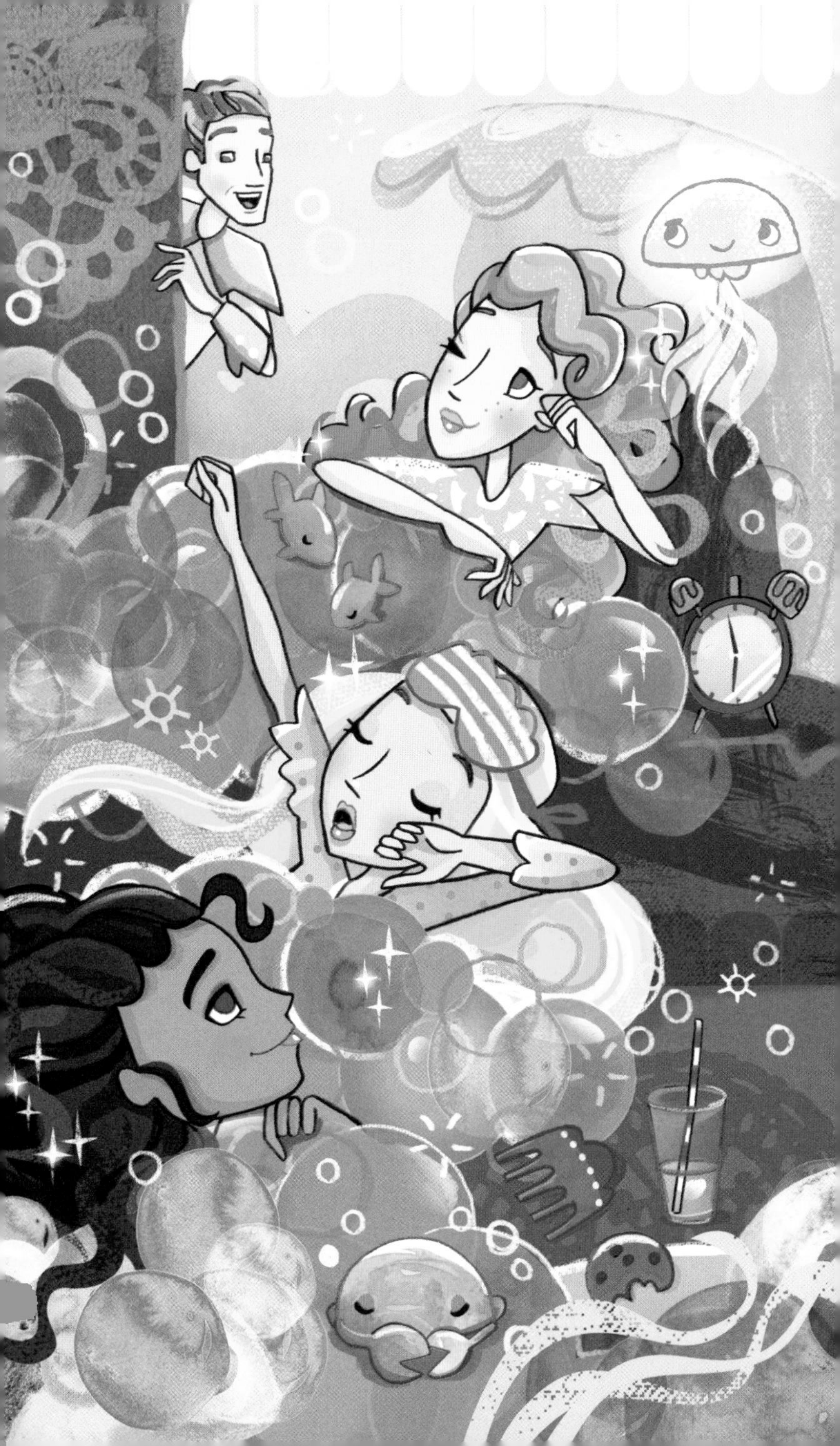

special meeting. She's a busy lady, and the only time she could meet with us was at eight this morning. So we have to get going. All of us! This is important. Lend the girls some sparkly tops and make sure you all look presentable."

Shyanna and Cora nodded, excited. It wasn't often that mermaids our age got to meet with the Queen in private.

"What's it about?" I asked him, glancing at my two friends, who looked equally puzzled.

"It's a secret." He wouldn't say anything more.

The girls and I jumped up out of bed and started to get ready while Dad made breakfast.

"I wonder what your dad is up to," Shyanna whispered.

I squeezed her hand. "I have no idea," I said. "All I know is that I'm sick of secrets."

Chapter Nine

The King and Queen's palace was so fancy! It was hard to believe Dad got to go there every day for work. Shyanna, Cora, and I giggled when the Queen's guard announced our names outside the private quarters. We tried our hardest not to freak out when they led us into the Queen's parlor.

The Queen was sitting on her throne, wearing a light purple cape. Her long blond hair was braided with sparkles and the fanciest pearls. She looked regal, proper, and perfect.

She stood and winked at us when we came in. "Look. It's my favorite warm-up singers and my coach!" she said. The nerves in my stomach melted. "You girls did such an amazing job at the concert. I'd like to do it again sometime!"

The Queen offered us some tea, and we sat at a table in front of her throne. There were large cookies with pink frosting on a plate on the table. It might have been early, but that didn't stop Shyanna from grabbing a cookie right away.

"Your majesty," my dad said, bowing his head. "I asked to speak with you today about a matter of extreme importance."

We all stared at Dad.

"As you know, my daughter, Rachel, is half-human," he continued.

"I am aware," the Queen said with a smile. "Her mother — your wife — was a wonderful mermaid, wife, mom, and friend. She took to our life so well. It was a pleasure to welcome her to our world with

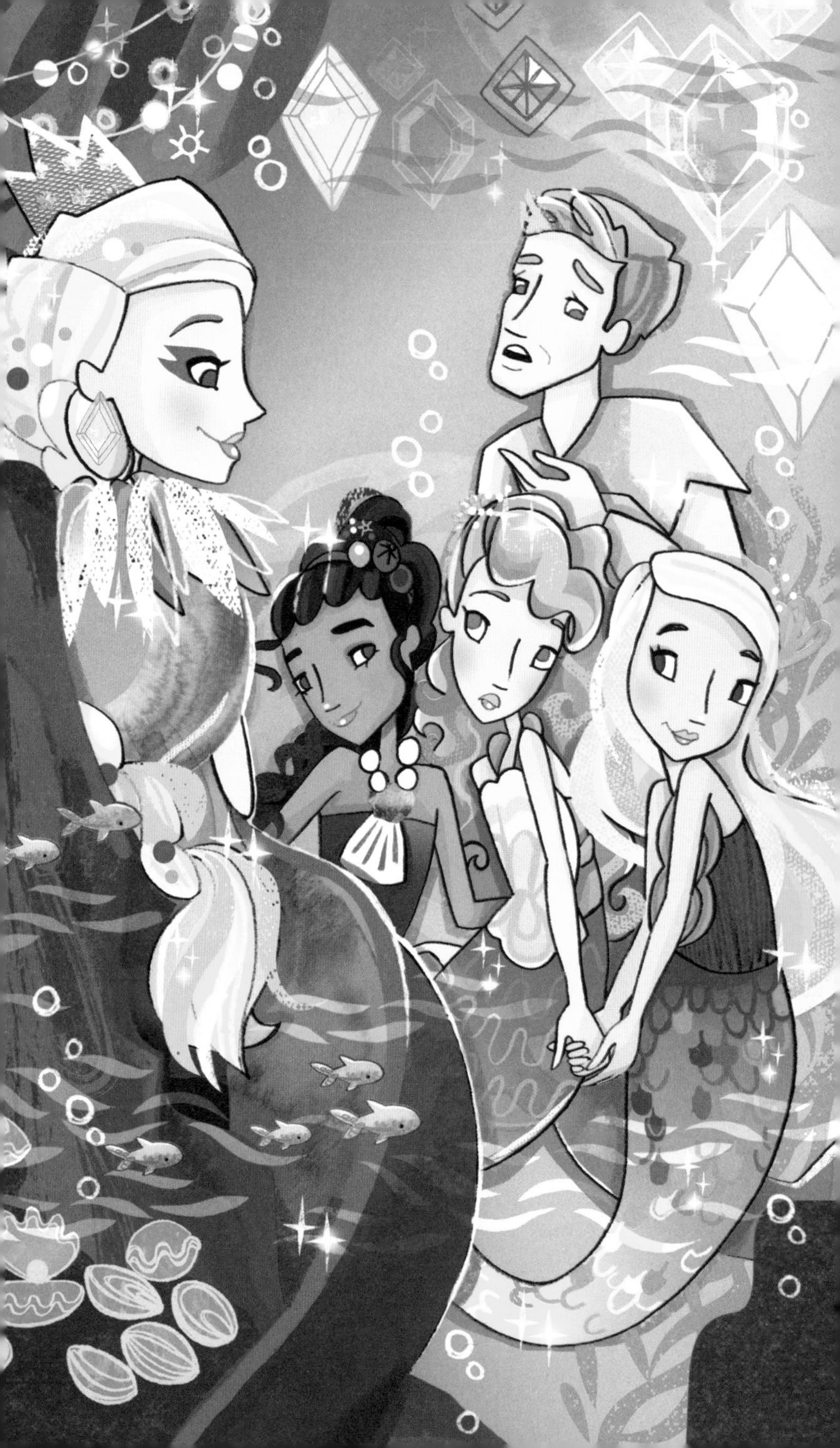

magic. It was one of the best decisions I have ever made. I am still so sorry for your loss."

"Thank you. We are too. We miss her every day," Dad said, looking down. Then he glanced at me. "This is what I came to discuss. The fact is that no recent mermaids in Neptunia have had human mothers. And in the past — in other kingdoms — Rachel has been teased for being half-human."

Cora and Shyanna each grabbed one of my hands and squeezed it tightly.

The Queen frowned, but my dad kept going. "Rachel can travel to land and stay there as long as she wants. I've allowed her to explore, and while on land she made a really special friend. A human."

The Queen nodded. "Owen," she said. "He is a good human."

My cheeks got a little warm.

"Don't look so surprised, Rachel," the Queen said. "We know about Owen. For your protection. We keep an eye on our mermaids, even when they're on land."

"Unfortunately," Dad said, "teasing is something Rachel never escapes. For that, among other reasons, she's expressed interest in becoming a human."

The Queen tilted her head and gazed at me with wide, sympathetic eyes. "Is that true?"

I nodded, unable to speak. Afraid.

"If you give up your tail, you can never get it back," the Queen said.

I swallowed, grateful the girls were holding my hands. I didn't want to think about giving up being a mermaid forever, but it seemed like the best solution. I wanted Owen to be a part of my life all the time. I wanted to have a normal life.

"I have a different solution," my dad said. "One that might make Rachel reconsider her choice."

We all stared at him. Even the Queen.

"What if we grant Owen temporary merman status to visit Rachel? He's thirteen, so he could do the same as mermaids do on land, only in reverse. A few hours in the ocean to see her life. And then

Rachel could share her friends and her world here with Owen. She wouldn't have to keep her real self a secret from him anymore."

"Exposure to humans is always risky," the Queen said, frowning.

"But my mom proved to be trustworthy!" I cried.

She raised her hand. "Let me finish, please."

I pressed my lips tightly.

"Owen has the right human qualities to be trusted," the Queen continued. "The question is, would having Owen visit keep you from wanting to turn to human form permanently?"

I nodded my head vigorously. Having Owen know the truth really would help. My dad was a genius.

"He would have to keep the secret," the Queen said. "And if he didn't, he would turn into a merman. He would never be able to return back to human form. His family would believe he was lost at sea. This is a delicate matter that must be taken very seriously. Do you understand what you are asking?"

I thought about Owen and how he always said there was nothing that could prevent him from being my friend. I knew he could be trusted. I nodded again.

"I do, and I know they are only teenagers," my dad said. "But I believe they have old souls and can be trusted. Their friendship is stronger than any I've ever witnessed."

The Queen sipped her tea and then put down her cup. "From what I've seen, I agree with your assessment. Their bond is incredible."

"Sometimes a strong friendship can be as strong as love," my dad said. "Wouldn't you agree, Queen?"

"I do. I really do," she said with a smile. "Rachel, you may tell Owen the truth. He can be brought here if he agrees. It is his choice. If he doesn't agree, he will forget what you've told him."

"Really?" I whispered. I was in shock.

"Once you tell him," the Queen explained, "you must be aware that if he chooses not to be part merman, you will no longer be allowed to visit him.

Too much exposure after that may wear off the mermaid magic, and he could eventually remember the truth about you. That cannot be allowed to happen."

I loved being a mermaid far too much to give it up. I knew in my heart that being different didn't mean being bad. If I could tell my best friend the truth and bring him to Neptunia to see my life here, it would be worth all the hassle. I was sure he wouldn't turn me down. I was so sure, I was willing to risk losing him forever.

I would tell Owen the truth and offer him a chance to see a life that other humans couldn't even imagine. The world beneath the sea. Having the four of us together would be a dream come true. Owen, Shyanna, Cora, and me!

I gulped and nodded at the Queen. She snapped her finger, and a mermaid appeared and gave me a magic pill. It would turn Owen into a merman.

If he chose to be one.

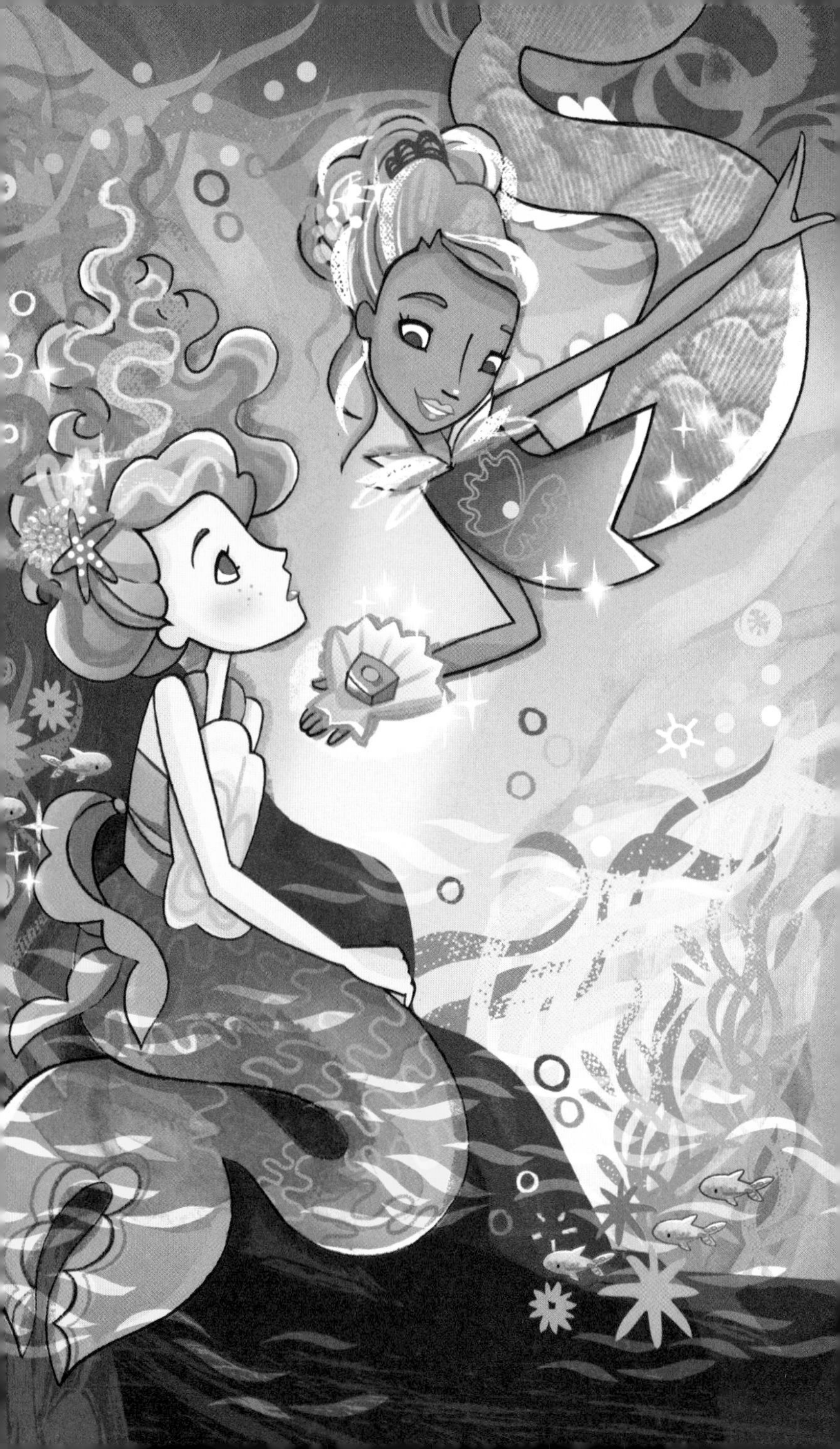

Chapter Ten

The next morning, Shyanna, Cora, and my dad each hugged me before I left to find Owen. I was beyond nervous. I couldn't believe it was really happening! It was like a dream.

I found Owen on shore in our special spot. I had sent Owen a text the night before, so I knew he'd be waiting for me. I didn't know how to tell him my secret, so I just blurted it out. When I finished telling him the truth, and the rules about knowing the truth and the choice he had to make, he didn't look upset at all. He didn't even look that surprised. I guess that is a normal boy response to most things.

"Mermaids," he said, smiling. "That's the coolest thing I've ever heard."

"You aren't mad or weirded out?" I asked.

"It's weird, but I always knew there was something different about you. Not weird different, but magical different."

"You did?" I asked.

"I think that's what brought us together. And of course I can keep it a secret. You're my best friend. And of course I want to see your world!"

My cheeks glowed with happiness. He looked back at me, and I saw that his cheeks were glowing too. He touched his neck, and I noticed he was wearing the shark tooth necklace I got him for his birthday. I touched the shell necklace he gave me, the one that I never took off.

For a moment I wondered if we'd ever be more than friends, but then I tucked that idea away. I didn't want to ruin what we had right now. A great friendship was more than I could ask for.

"Merpeople," he said as we walked toward the ocean. "I always wondered why you were constantly on the beach, but you would never swim." He pointed at my legs. "I can't wait to see your tail!"

"I can't wait to see yours!" I told him, and we both stared down at his legs.

"Me neither!" he yelled, and then he started to run toward the water.

"Wait!" I called and laughed.

"You have to take this first," I said as I pulled out the magic pill the Queen gave me. "You are sure about all of this? You don't need to think about it longer or anything?"

He nodded. "Are you crazy? I can't wait!"

"Okay. Then take this, and we'll go to Neptunia to meet my friends," I said.

He swallowed the pill. "Tastes like fish," he said, smiling. He stared down at his legs, waiting.

I laughed and pulled him into the ocean. My tail spread down, shimmering in the sunshine.

"Wow!" he said, his eyes sparkling in amazement.

And then we both watched as his tail spread down until his legs disappeared and a tail took their place. It was a glorious tail, reds and oranges twinkling in the water. He whooped loudly, and then we dove down under a wave. The grin didn't leave his face. He was an amazing swimmer and took to his fins right away.

Owen was like a little kid, stopping to admire every shellfish and jellyfish and waving lobster. He played with the dolphins that came to greet us, and the grumpy old whale that swam by and blew a spout of water made him laugh.

When we finally arrived at Neptunia, Shyanna and Cora were waiting in Walrus Waterpark for us. They looked as happy as me and Owen. The girls hugged Owen like he was an old friend. And it was then I knew that this was the right choice.

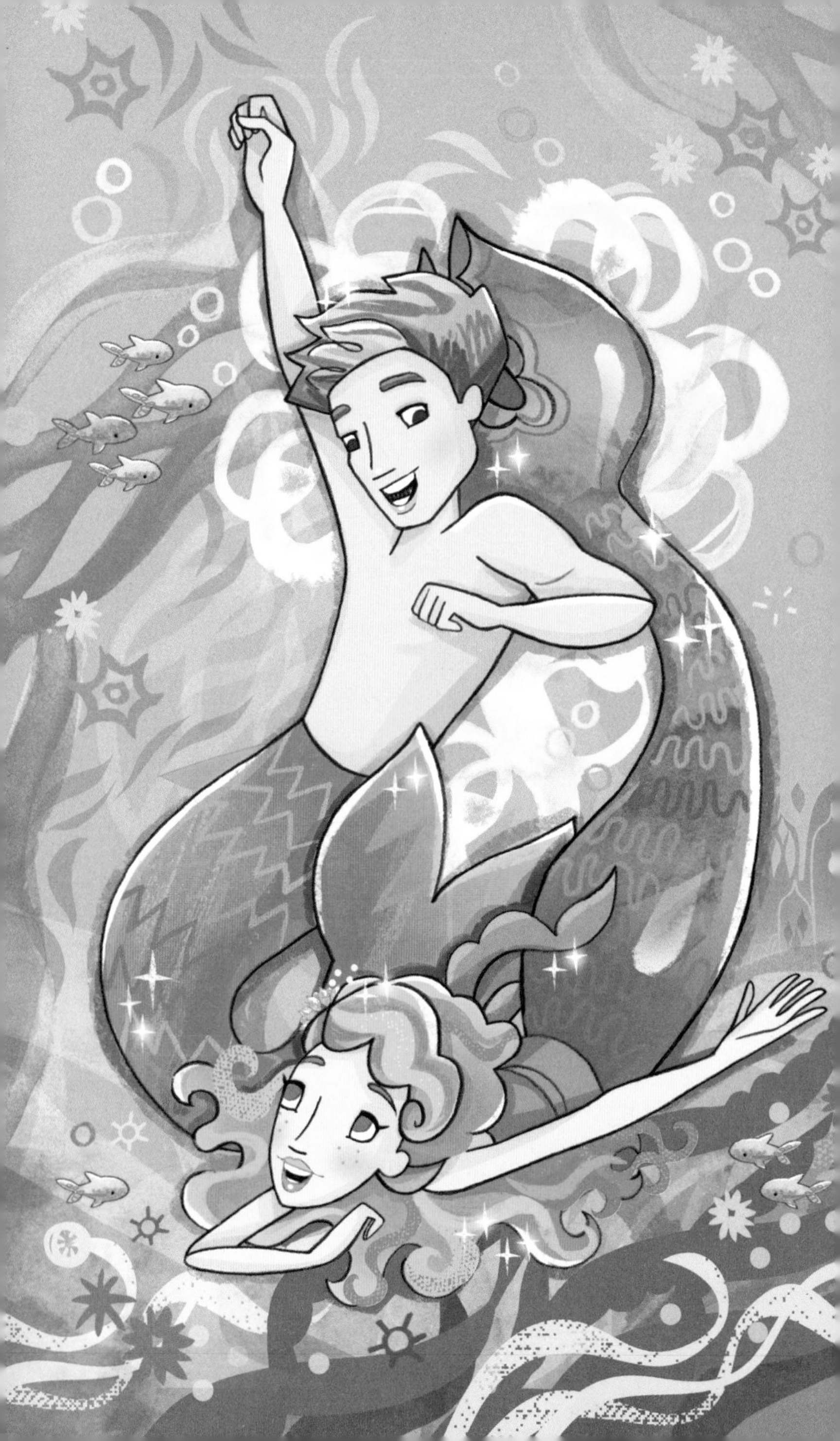

But soon, we weren't the only merpeople at Walrus Waterpark. Regina and a group of her mermaid friends arrived.

"Who is this?" Regina asked, swimming closer.

"I'm Owen," he said, not intimidated. "And this is my best friend, Rachel, and my new friends Shyanna and Cora. We're merpeople!"

We all laughed at his enthusiasm.

"I know what we are," Regina said, turning her nose up a bit. But he also intrigued her, I could tell. "Where did you come from?"

He winked at her. "That's kind of a secret between friends. Do you mind?" he asked, and then he twirled up and did a double flip turn. "I have to say, I like Neptunia a lot. You'd better get used to seeing me around."

Regina was not smiling. I had a feeling I was going to have to deal with her a lot once school started, but I didn't care. Having Owen here was worth dealing with Regina.

She swam away, with her friends following behind. I grabbed Owen's hand. His time was almost up already, and we had to get him back to land. "Come on, Owen, we have to get going," I said.

"We're so glad we got to meet you!" Shyanna said.

"And we'll come visit you on shore once we turn thirteen and get our legs!" Cora added.

We were all excited to add a fourth best friend to our friendship circle. "Come on, Owen," I said to him. "Let's go to shore. You can come back and visit soon!"

"Just try to keep me away," he said.

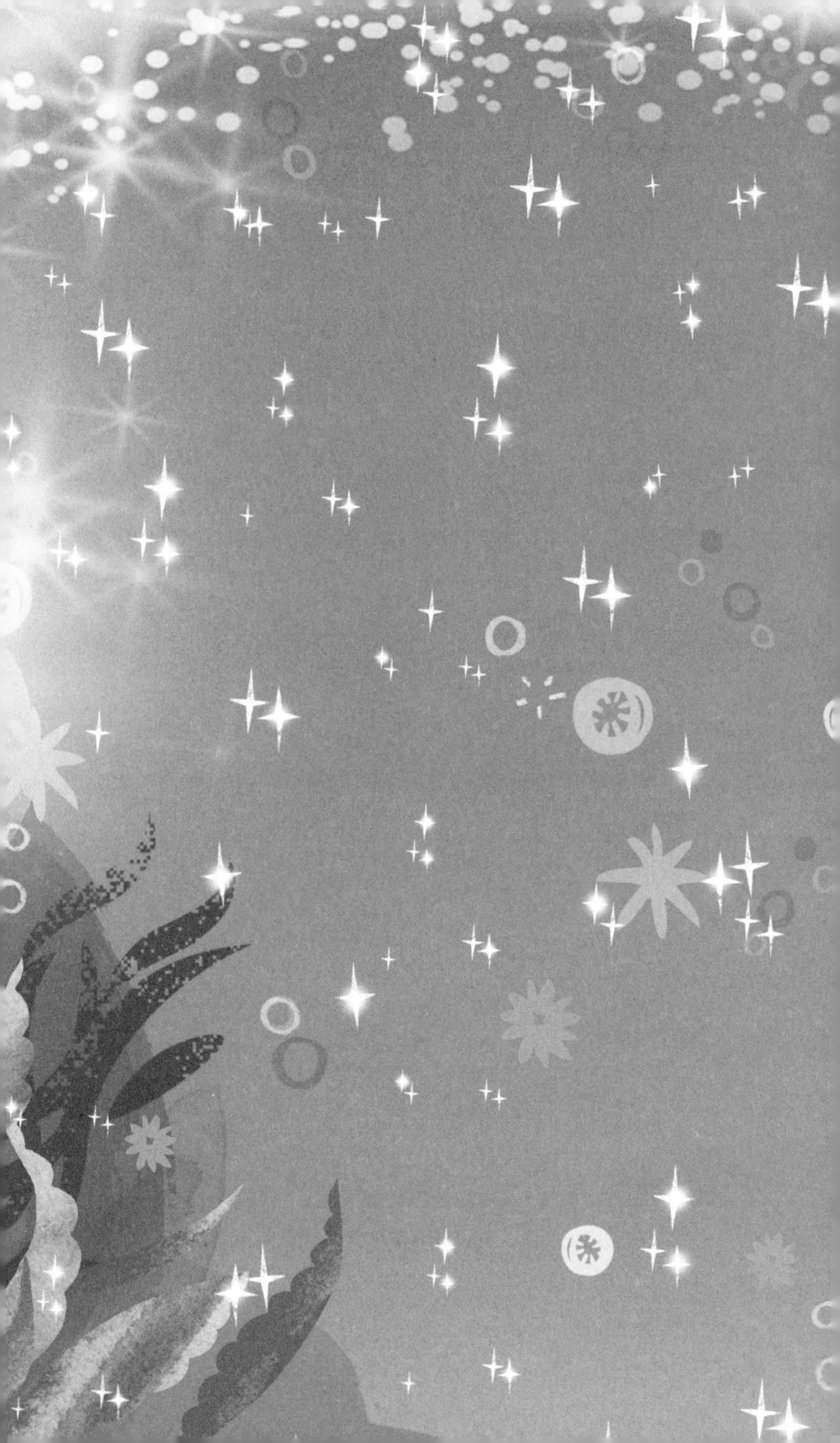

Legend of Mermaids

These creatures of the sea have many secrets. Although people have believed in mermaids for centuries, nobody has ever proven their existence. People all over the world are attracted to the mysterious mermaids.

The earliest mermaid story dates back to around 1000 BC in an Assyrian legend. A goddess loved a human man but killed him accidentally. She fled to the water in shame. She tried to change into a fish, but the water would not let her hide her true nature. She lived the rest of her days as half-woman, half-fish.

Later, the ancient Greeks whispered tales of fishy women called sirens. These beautiful but deadly beings lured sailors to their graves. Many sailors feared or respected mermaids because of their association with doom.

Note: This text was taken from The Girl's Guide to Mermaids: Everything Alluring about These Mythical Beauties *by Sheri A. Johnson (Capstone Press, 2012). For more mermaid facts, be sure to check this book out!*

Talk It Out

1. Before Rachel moved to Neptunia, she was teased at her old school. Teasing is a type of bullying, which is never okay. Talk about a time when you felt bullied. How did you handle it?

2. Were you surprised by Cora's reaction when she found out Rachel's secret? How about Owen's reaction? How do you think you would have reacted?

3. Friendship is a special type of love. What qualities make a good friend? How are those qualities shown in this story?

4. What would you have done if you were Owen? Would you have said yes to Rachel's request so easily?

Write It Down

1. Pretend you are Rachel. Make a pro and con list to support your decision to tell Owen your big secret.

2. Rachel missed her mom. Write a letter to your mom or an important person in your life. You can choose to give it to them or keep it for yourself.

3. Rachel was half-human, which made her different. Our differences are what make us unique. Write a paragraph about your unique qualities and how they make you special.

4. Write an alternate ending for the story. Maybe Owen says no to Rachel's request, or Regina follows Rachel and tells everyone her secret. It's your ending, so finish the story any way you want.

About the Author

Janet Gurtler has written numerous well-received YA books. Mermaid Kingdom is her debut series for younger readers. She lives in Calgary, Alberta, near the Canadian Rockies, with her husband, son, and a chubby Chihuahua named Bruce. Gurtler does not live in an igloo or play hockey, but she does love maple syrup and says "eh" a lot.

About the Illustrator

Katie Wood fell in love with drawing
when she was very small. Since graduating
from Loughborough University School of
Art and Design in 2004, she has been living
her dream working as a freelance illustrator.
From her studio in Leicester, England, she
creates bright and lively illustrations for
books and magazines all over the world.

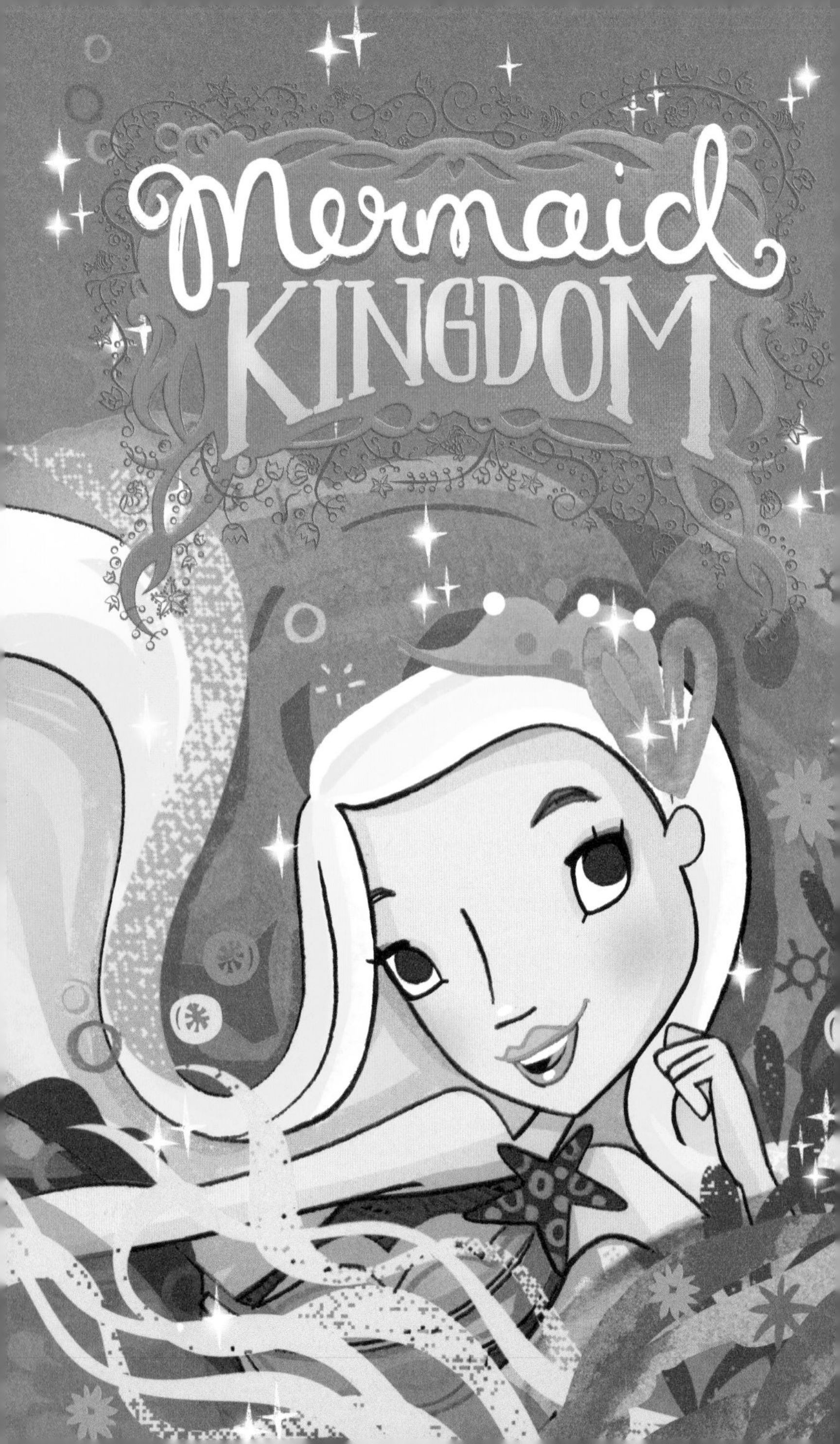
Mermaid
KINGDOM

Dive in and get swept away!

Mermaid KINGDOM
by Janet Gurtler

Shyanna's Song

Mermaid KINGDOM
by Janet Gurtler

Rachel's Secret

Mermaid KINGDOM
by Janet Gurtler

Cora's Decision

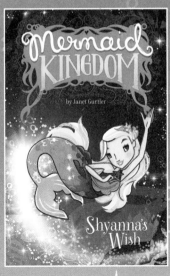

Mermaid KINGDOM
by Janet Gurtler

Shyanna's Wish

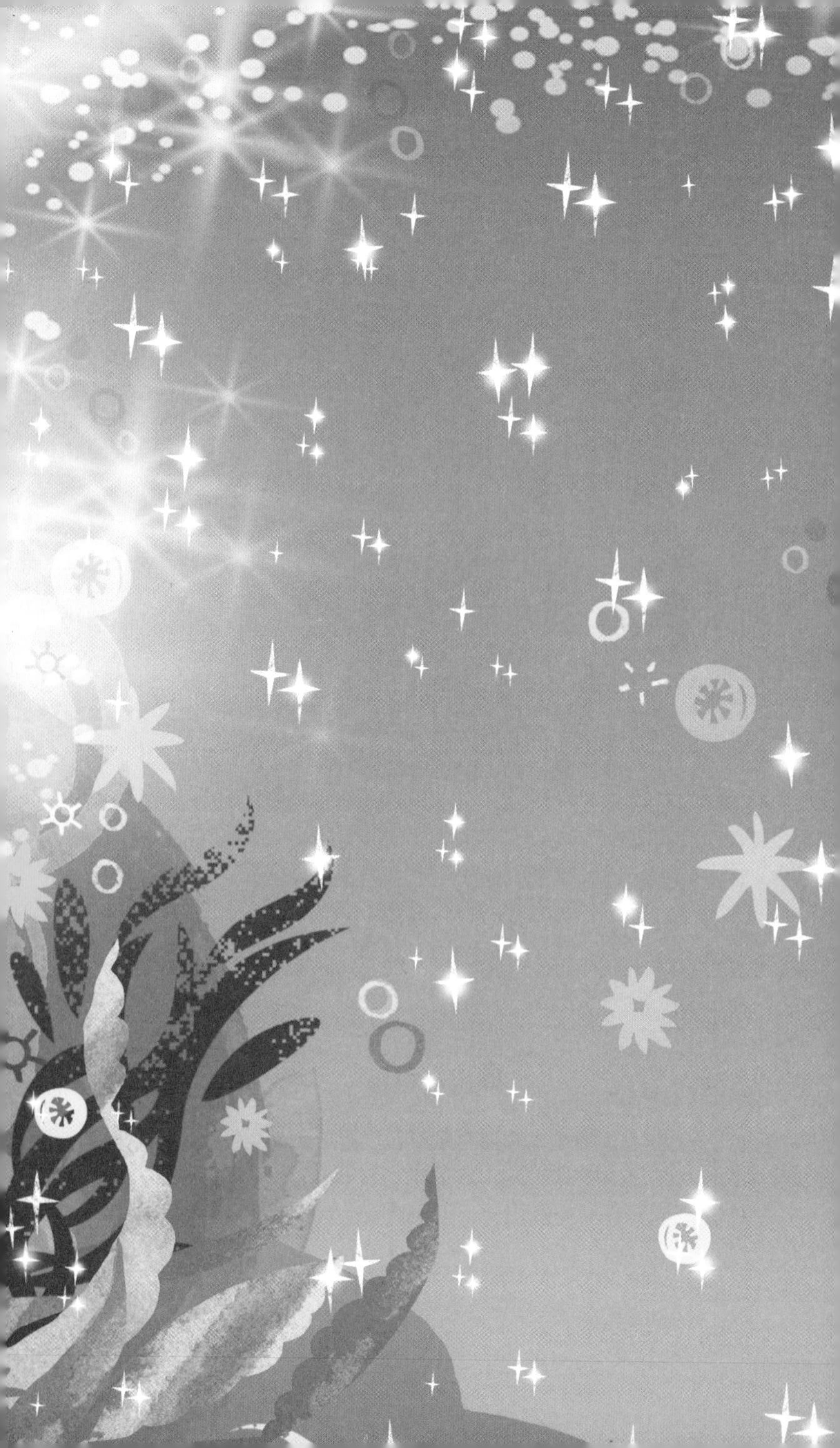

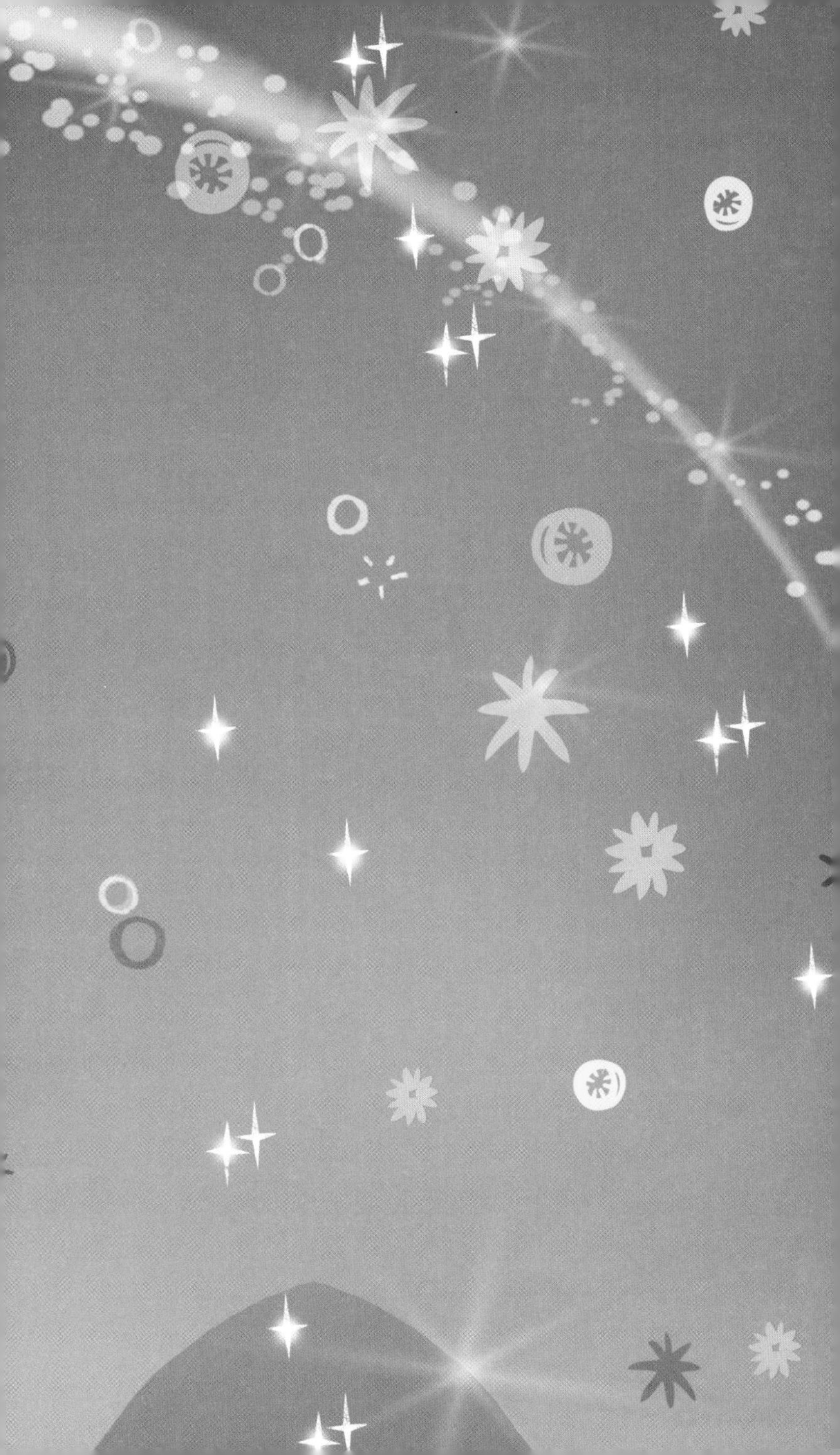